THE
ZOMBIE
STONE

ALSO BY K. G. CAMPBELL

A Small Zombie Problem

THE ZOMBIE STONE

ZOMBIE PROBLEMS
BOOK 2

K. G. CAMPBELL

ALFRED A. KNOPF
NEW YORK

THIS IS A BORZOI BOOK PUBLISHED BY ALFRED A. KNOPF

Visit us on the Web! rhcbooks.com

Educators and librarians, for a variety of teaching tools, visit us at RHTeachersLibrarians.com

Library of Congress Cataloging-in-Publication Data is available upon request.
ISBN 978-1-101-93159-2 (trade) — ISBN 978-1-101-93160-8 (lib. bdg.) — ISBN 978-1-101-93161-5 (ebook)

The text of this book is set in 12-point Simoncini Garamond.
The illustrations were created using watercolor and colored pencil.
Interior design by Stephanie Moss

Printed in the United States of America
January 2021
10 9 8 7 6 5 4 3 2 1
First Edition

*To Debbie and Rick, who
inspired the whole thing*

CONTENTS

PART I

PART II

PART I

CHAPTER 1

THE FOUNDERING VESSEL—PART 1

It had become apparent that the canoe was sinking.

The opaque brown water, which had moments before been sloshing around the boy's shoes, had now reached his ankles.

"Claudette!" cried the boy urgently, pointing toward the largest of several spouting holes. "Stop that up with your finger!"

The girl named Claudette, however, must surely have been stronger than she realized. For while attempting to plug the gushing water, she promptly forced her entire fist through the vessel's hull, dramatically worsening the situation, as you might imagine.

The boy scrambled across the canoe to stuff the jagged gash with a plaid blanket. But within moments the wool was a saturated lump, the "repair" worthless, and, in the meantime, more leaks were appearing. Indeed, with every second, there was more and more water, and less and less canoe.

As wet coldness reached his knees, the boy finally came to understand that the boat was doomed.

Yet even then, he did not fully appreciate the dire nature of his predicament.

There was, however, someone who did.

One hundred feet above the foundering vessel, an osprey was headed back to its nest and family with a freshly caught bass. The bird observed the splashy drama far below with a detached curiosity, as you or I might observe some feathery calamity in the sky above.

The male human, just visible through a cloud of tasty-looking butterflies, had removed his oddly netted helmet and, for some reason, was using it to toss around water. The female human—who moved like a thing living, but to the bird above smelled like a thing dead—was with cupped hands, awkwardly attempting to do the same.

Humans, the osprey mused, were an odd bunch. What the frantic pair were trying to achieve he could hardly imagine. But what he spied next, the osprey understood only too well; for every creature of the swamp is hardwired to recognize the most dangerous of predators.

Through the watery channel, just beneath the surface, moved the pale shadow of a white beast. So enormous was it that the osprey dropped its family's dinner in shock. The thing was wider than the vessel was long, and its powerful, snaking tail created a wake like that of a shrimp boat.

And the white, enormous, snaking beast with a powerful wake was rapidly advancing upon the sinking canoe.

CHAPTER 2

OUTSIDE THE BUTTERFLY BUFFER ZONE

But before we discover the fate of August and Claudette DuPont (for such were the names of the children in that ill-fated craft), we must return to the previous day, when the events leading to this remarkable situation began in a pretty unremarkable way.

August DuPont popped his head around the kitchen door, where his aunt Hydrangea was counting bottles of DuPont's Peppy Pepper Sauce as she placed them into a cardboard box.

"Eleven, twelve, thirteen," muttered the wide-eyed lady in the pink tiara. She cast about the kitchen table, then, skirts rustling, turned entirely around, scanning the room. "That can't be all. It surely can't be all. I could have sworn . . ."

"I'm just heading outside, Aunt," August announced, "to fertilize the pepper plants." Hydrangea, distracted, was conducting a recount.

"Is it," she inquired absently, "the right time of year for such a measure, sugar?"

August slid a book into the lady's line of sight.

The volume was rather old, of the hard-backed variety that was printed before the invention of dust jackets. Its elaborate title and cover decoration were embossed and gilded, but the edges were fraying, the leaf wearing thin, and the pages were scarcely held together by the spine.

"It is the right time," August assured his aunt, donning long, bulky gloves and a netted beekeeper's helmet, "according to LouLou Bouquet."

Wistfully, Hydrangea placed her fingers on the book.

"Now, where," she wondered, "did you ever find this old thing?"

"It's been helping to prop up my desk," responded August. "The one with the broken leg. I noticed it a while back, when I was looking for a pushpin on the floor."

Hydrangea lifted the volume.

"The Capsicum Compendium," she read. *"A Practical Pocket Guide for the Professional Pepper Planter."* She looked up. "You know, sugar, that in over one hundred years, no one has produced a more learned or reliable manual on pepper farming?

Or so my papa would say. He regarded Miz Bouquet's authority on the subject as absolute. So did his papa. And his."

She handed the book to August, a faint crease in her brow.

"And now you pick up the torch, the last of the DuPonts. Perhaps you, August, can one day revive the family hot sauce empire. Have I ever told you that DuPont's Peppy Pepper Sauce was once the most highly regarded—"

"—hot sauce in the world?" August had heard this speech so many times before, he could finish it verbatim. "From Croissant City to Paris, France. Fiery yet sweet. Like a dragon's kiss."

Hydrangea laid her hand on the boy's cheek and smiled sadly.

"I'm glad to see at least," she said, "that LouLou Bouquet is being put to more fitting use than supporting broken furniture."

Awkwardly, as he was holding a book in his gloved hand, August heaved a generously-sized sack of fertilizer from the kitchen floor.

"Now remember, sugar," said Hydrangea. "No further—"

"I know, ma'am," interrupted August shortly. "No further than the gate."

"Can't you content yourself, child, with the yard?" Hydrangea's voice had an injured air of appeal. "It's true that Locust Hole is not the place it once was, but it is by no means a small property. There is fresh air, a canal to fish, trees to climb."

The lady pursed her lips.

"You may well roll your eyes, August. But let us not forget that your last misadventure into the cruel world has left us with ongoing"—lowering her voice, she glanced at the ceiling—"consequences."

In the foyer, August stopped to slide LouLou Bouquet's compendium under his bag-wielding arm, thus freeing a hand to open the front door. As his gloved fist slid over the smooth brass, he paused, recalling the very first time he ever turned it, eight months before.

Only eight months had passed since the boy had stepped beyond the threshold of his house for the first time. He glanced at the wood plank barricades resting redundant against the foyer wall, and recalled lifting them from their brackets, gingerly so as not to alert his high-strung aunt.

So petrified was the lady, of butterflies and betrayals and almost everything else in the world beyond Locust Hole, she had sought to keep her nephew safely sheltered within its walls.

Sliding through the front door and closing it firmly behind him, the boy crossed a screened-in porch and navigated voluminous net curtains to arrive at the crisp spring air and sunlight beyond.

The bag of fertilizer landed with a dull thump in the dirt of a planter, beside some weedy green shoots, the yard's only living plants. The circular flowerbed lay at the center of a geometric pattern that had once represented an Italian garden. But the small hedges defining the paths had long since perished, the gravel was thin and scattered, and the Grecian urns lay prone and broken.

Swatting aside three butterflies that had immediately fluttered into orbit around him, August crouched and examined a seedling, lifting a limp leaf.

"No fruit yet, you guys?" he sighed. "I know it's only March, but I'd really hoped to surprise Aunt Hydrangea today with some tiny babies. But you're looking sadder than a catfish in a soup pot. Maybe LouLou Bouquet can tell me what I'm doing wrong." The boy placed the book on the bag of fertilizer. "But I'm afraid that she will have to wait."

August straightened, glanced toward the house, then strode quickly toward the yard gate. To the left of it, atop a crooked post, perched a mailbox. The rusty arch-topped receptacle had a door at either end, to deposit or retrieve its contents from yard or street.

In a single, swift movement, August removed an envelope from his pocket and placed it inside. It was more of a struggle, however, to raise the tin flag that indicated the presence of outgoing mail; clearly many years had passed since the thing was moved.

"I hope," thought August, "that Mr. LaPoste notices the

flag. He usually picks up our mail from the porch, but I think it should catch his eye."

The boy shot another glance over his shoulder. Nothing. He rubbed his palms on his thighs. "She didn't see," he thought. "Good."

Mission accomplished, the boy's shoulders relaxed, and he was about to turn back toward the fertilizer and LouLou Bouquet when a sound stopped him short. It was the weak, crispy-crunchy roll of bicycle tires.

"Grosbeak's!"

Holding the pointed ends of the pickets to shield his ribs, August leaned over the gate, craning to catch a glimpse of the approaching rider. He wondered if it would be the same girl as last time. August had enjoyed the way her long, bony legs stuck out every which way, making him think of a grasshopper on a bike.

But it seemed unlikely. No one ever delivered to Locust Hole more than once. At least, not since Gaston.

August couldn't help but feel nostalgic for the sturdy red-headed delivery boy who had, with well-devised bait, lured him out into the world beyond Locust Hole for the first time.

The trap had launched a tumultuous period, filled with problems large and small. But it had also been a time of great happiness; a time when August had believed himself to have friends. He revisited the heartwarming sense of belonging he had enjoyed when, very briefly, his life had resembled that of his favorite TV teen, Stella Starz.

But, with a sickening lurch of the heart, he forced himself back to reality.

In the end, he thought, he'd been wrong. There were no friends. Only deception and betrayal. He ran his fingers over the dent in his helmet, a battle scar from the catastrophe that had smashed his newfound joy to bits.

But August was, like his helmet, only dented, not destroyed. He was young and resilient and, despite all his misfortunes, filled with hope.

"Perhaps," he contemplated, brightening at the prospect, "grasshopper girl watches *Stella Starz (in Her Own Life)*. I wonder if she's seen the cat litter commercial with Officer Claw, Stella's cat. Maybe she likes Mudd Pies." Armed with these compelling questions, August braced himself to open a conversation.

The bicycle's rider, however, was not the grasshopper-like girl, but a smallish, wiry boy. He dismounted, his uneasy, bulging eyes glued to the house. So engrossed was he that he didn't even notice August's beekeeper gloves, nor his dented helmet, nor the five butterflies circling it.

"Did you bring," asked August, "the fiberglass patches and glue that my aunt ordered?" Without removing his gaze from the front porch, the boy wordlessly handed two brown paper bags over the gate.

"Yep! Here they are," said August with satisfaction, discovering the desired items near the top of one bag. He looked up with a forced smile.

"Have you," he launched in brightly, "by any chance, seen the commercial for Kitty Clumps with Stella Starz's cat, Officer Claw?"

But before any discussion could commence, August heard the front door slam behind him, the swish of net curtain, and dragging, heavy footsteps on the porch steps.

He watched the delivery boy's expression turn from apprehension to undisguised horror. August's shoulders slumped; he sighed and closed his eyes, awaiting what he knew would happen next.

It happened every time.

The boy opened his mouth, pointed at something over August's shoulder, and screamed, "Zombie!"

CHAPTER 3

INSIDE THE BUTTERFLY BUFFER ZONE

"Take these," grumbled August, shoving the grocery bags into Claudette's arms. Claudette was August's great-great-aunt who had died many years ago at nine years old. Much more recently, she had happened to become undead, and had proved to be problematic ever since, particularly when it came to August's quest to make friends.

"Do something useful," snapped August, "rather than just scaring off kids, would you?" Upon seeing the zombie's doleful expression, the boy regretted his irritated tone. "I know you didn't mean to," he said, offering up a conciliatory smile.

Passing back into the screened-in porch, August unhooked a butterfly net from a nail on the wall and launched into a bizarre dance, darting about and swiftly spinning around to capture the confused insects within the net. Having caught and released two of them through the screen curtain, August glanced around the porch.

"All clear," he announced, propping open the front door and catching a carton of eggs as Claudette lurched indoors.

"We need," August hissed, taking one of the bags from the zombie, "to find that Zombie Stone. I still can't believe Aunt Orchid sold it. Although to be fair, she didn't know it was the marble in my skeleton model. But then, neither did I when I gave the model to her. Somehow, though, we have to track it down; it's the only way to return you to the land of the dead, where you belong. It will be best," he added reassuringly, "for everyone."

As they entered the kitchen, Hydrangea was turning on the television.

"You didn't," she said, looking up with vague alarm, "permit any butterflies—"

"To enter?" interrupted August. "No ma'am. The butterfly buffer zone is functioning just as intended."

"Clever boy." Hydrangea smiled with pride. "Ah, Grosbeak's has delivered. Did they include the things you asked for, the materials you need for those funny models of yours?"

"They did, thank you," responded August. "I have enough now, I think, to finish the pirate ship."

"Pirates, hmm. That's nice, sugar." Hydrangea was only half listening as she lowered herself onto a wooden settee, plumping a threadbare cushion behind her. "Hush now, my favorite educational show is starting."

The room immediately filled with the melodic voice of a television presenter, who introduced herself as Dixie Lispings and welcomed the audience to . . .

". . . another envy-inducing episode of *Absurdly Opulent Homes of the Very Rich and Even Richer*."

"Educational show?" questioned August wryly, throwing Claudette a discreet smile.

"One can, you know, learn a great deal about history and architect—aaaaaargh!"

August nearly dropped his paper sack when Hydrangea let out a sudden, strangled howl. He spun around to see her slack-jawed, one hand gripping the arm of the settee, the other pointing a shaking finger at the television.

"This week," Dixie cheerfully informed her viewers, "we're in the charming Old Quarter of vibrant Croissant City. This sumptuous townhouse behind me at 591 Funeral Street is the pied-à-terre of the Malveau family. And yes, I do mean Malveau, as in world-famous Malveau's Devil Sauce."

"The Malveau family?" muttered August, depositing his bag safely on the counter and wandering toward the television.

"The Malveau family?" repeated Hydrangea with shrill outrage. "That house belongs to us! It has done, for generations." Then, more quietly, "At least . . . it used to."

"To us?" August inquired, baffled.

"Another chunk of the family legacy," lamented Hydrangea, gesturing at the screen with her handkerchief, "stolen away by our archrivals. Stolen by those who would see the DuPonts and DuPont's Peppy Pepper Sauce wiped from the earth. Stolen by the Malveaus!" She glanced at August's skeptically arched brow. "Well, bought," she admitted reluctantly. "But for a shockingly low sum." She turned again to the television and gave the hankie a vigorous twisting.

"Given Orchid's designs on the DuPont treasure, you know, Orfeo's Cadaverite, I wouldn't be at all surprised if she acquired the property solely in the hope of discovering the thing somewhere inside." She lifted the remote and turned up the volume.

"Oh look, sugar, they've re-papered the entry hall. I suppose it was growing quite shabby the last time I saw it. But the chandeliers are a bit much, don't you think? And so much gold. How vulgar."

Hydrangea was clearly lost now, to the show and to her own resentment. So, August quietly lifted some items from the grocery bag, nudged Claudette, and nodded toward the kitchen door.

* * *

The sun was setting and the temperature dropping as the boy and the zombie pushed past the cluster of spiky palmettos behind the old, ruined gazebo.

On a narrow strip of sandy mud at the edge of the canal, hidden from the house by the plants and garden structure, rested a canoe. The wooden vessel was peppered with square patches, hardened goo peeking from their edges.

August removed his bulky gloves and rummaged in his pockets. He turned to Claudette, holding up the bag of fiberglass patches and a tube of marine epoxy.

"Finally, Claudette," he whispered with a grin, "this will be the last one. After all these months of smuggling it in, bit by bit. Aunt Hydrangea believes it's all just supplies for my sculptures." He raised his eyebrows. "She thinks I'm building a model ship for a crew of pirate skeletons. Imagine if she knew we're repairing the sunken canoe you rescued from the bottom of the canal."

Crouching down, the boy shook a wafer-thin square from the bag, placed it on the ground, and squeezed the special glue around its edges.

"I reckon it would have been quicker," he considered, "to take the bus." He shook his head, applying the patch to the canoe, pressing it gently around the edges with his index finger. "But that takes money, and Aunt Hydrangea doesn't have much to spare. I don't want to take a penny more than we absolutely need." He sat back to admire his handiwork. A shadow of concern passed across his face.

"I do hope she'll be okay, Claudette," he said with an air of uncertainty.

He pulled an envelope from his pocket and glanced at the zombie.

"You know she'd never give us permission to go. I wrote her this note to explain. And I wrote another one to the mailman, Mr. LaPoste, asking him to take care of her while I'm gone. I left his in the mailbox today. Because, Claudette, we're leaving tonight. After I've glued on this last patch, we're going to find the Zombie Stone."

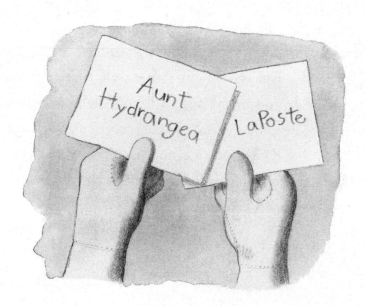

CHAPTER 4

THE FOUNDERING VESSEL—PART 2

And so it was that August and Claudette DuPont came to arrive at the place we found them: in a sinking canoe, upon a canal piercing Lost Souls' Swamp.

This less-than-perfect situation was indeed a disappointment, as the day had started out rather well. Claudette was an uncommonly vigorous rower and had propelled the vessel without interval from early morning to early evening. Such was the sight of a small girl powering a canoe faster than a fan boat that the voyage had been drawing looks of openmouthed amazement from passing pelicans and fishermen.

"We're making excellent progress, Claudette," said August encouragingly from the front of the canoe, glancing over his shoulder. The boy took a bite from the Mudd Pie he held in his left hand and consulted the foldout map in his right. "Black River is long behind us. This is, let's see, Channel Fifteen B. Only a few more miles to Pirate's Pier, then through the lock and we'll be on the Continental River.

"Hey! Why are my feet wet?"

August realized suddenly that water was collecting in the bottom of the canoe, and that several of his handcrafted patches had sprung leaks.

Leaning over the side, he could see that Claudette was powering the craft with such speed that the adhesive was no match for the rush of passing water, and the thin fiberglass veneers were being peeled away from the hull like old Band-Aids.

"Stop rowing! Stop!" cried August, grabbing his knapsack and hurriedly unearthing a tube of epoxy. But his efforts to repair the leaks were in vain. The fresh glue would not adhere to the wet wood, and several of the patches were, in any case, below the water line, where the epoxy was useless.

August splashed about the canoe, frantically squeezing and pressing. But the dribbles were growing into trickles. The trickles were growing into rivulets. Suddenly one patch popped a spout that arched across the benches and struck Claudette right in the face.

You have already heard what happened next. In her attempt

to stop up the offending hole, the zombie, miscalculating her own strength, forced not only her finger but her entire fist through the canoe's brittle shell.

Even a thick blanket could not stem the breach, and water was rapidly filling the vessel.

"Bail!" yelled August, whipping off his helmet and desperately scooping water from the boat. Claudette, panicked and confused, stumbled about with cupped hands, attempting to assist, but with highly limited results.

As he felt cold wetness around his knees, August straightened, and his predicament was immediately clear.

The front of the canoe was completely submerged. One oar was floating several yards away and out of reach. Nearby, the boy's knapsack was sliding beneath the canal's surface.

"The canoe is done for, Claudette," announced the boy. "Zombies can swim, right?"

But before Claudette could respond, something in the river beyond her caught August's eye. It was jagged and glittery, and moving swiftly through the ripples.

In one horrifying millisecond, August realized that the swift, jagged, glittery thing represented the back of an alligator.

But this was like no amphibious reptile August had seen in the informative game shows like *Win It or Lick It* that had constituted his education.

He could see the ghostly form of the beast beneath the water's surface. It was pure white. And it was immense: the width of a fishing boat, the length of a train car.

And it was getting even bigger. Quickly.

For the behemoth was headed directly for the foundering canoe.

CHAPTER 5

IN THE JAWS OF AN ALLIGATOR

A sudden piercing, high-pitched sound jerked August's head around.

Speeding toward him, engine sputtering and blue smoke spewing, was a very familiar, crudely built, perilously pitched houseboat. As it swung around, a scrawny, barefoot girl with a tangle of unbrushed hair came into view. She was manning the tiller and blowing fiercely into a long, elaborate brass whistle.

"Madame Marvell!" cried August, surprised and greatly relieved to see the girl who had spent the previous summer moored in the canal behind Locust Hole, the girl he had called the wild child before learning her name (or at least the name she went by, having forgotten her own).

But Madame Marvell was still yards away, and the alligator was closing in. August's head snapped frantically back and forth as he gauged the distances of rescue vessel and giant predator, approaching from opposite directions.

Only the canoe's stern was now visible, and August, farther forward than Claudette, was now thigh deep in water.

Three yards away, the alligator's rough-skinned snout broke the surface, close enough that August could see vapor snort from its nostrils and two yellow, reptilian eyes staring directly into his own. And, for the briefest of moments, August experienced some vague sense of recognition, as if he'd gazed into these eyes before.

Madame Marvell killed her engine, and the houseboat's pontoon glided close to the half-submerged canoe. Within seconds, the young pilot was hanging over the water, one hand clutching a rope for support, the other reaching out for August. But the girl was small, and the boy was lower than the houseboat's deck. The rapidly sinking canoe provided August with no static surface from which to push off.

As August's fingers wiggled merely inches from Marvell's, the boy saw something in the girl's face that made his stomach lurch; it was terror.

And in that same moment, from the corner of his eye, he spied massive jaws opening to reveal a shockingly pink interior with a flexing black gullet at its center.

Sunlight sparkled upon a horror show of dripping, razor-sharp teeth, each the size of an ice-cream cone, and August was enveloped by hot breath, rank with the stench of river swill and rotting fish.

The boy was wondering what it was going to feel like to be swallowed whole, when, with an otherworldly howl, Claudette the zombie hurled herself from the canoe's stern right into him, propelling him up and out. August felt Marvell's hand close around his wrist, and then the rough, hard planks of the deck beneath his knees. The whole world lurched with a deafening roar and splintering crash, as an immense flat head smashed through the houseboat's pontoon, missing August by mere inches.

The boy scrambled across the deck to brace his back against the houseboat's cabin (which, in a previous existence, had been a garden shed), preparing for a second assault.

But none came.

Wide-eyed, heart pounding, August stared at Madame Marvell, who clung to the generator with a similarly shell-shocked expression.

As the wild rocking subsided, August cautiously stood, recovered his helmet, and, grabbing whatever he could to steady himself, scanned the canal for the attacker.

But in the water beside the houseboat, only ripples remained.

The alligator was gone.
So was the canoe.
And so was Claudette.

CHAPTER 6

A DISMEMBERED LIMB

"Did you see that thing?" cried Madame Marvell. "You were lucky I came along just then; what would have become of you? Where has it gone? How could it just disappear? Are you okay?"

August did not respond but gazed down at the quieting waters.

"Claudette?" he called, almost fearfully.

Marvell joined him, and the pair stood in silence. Nothing appeared.

The children heard the plaintive *scree* of an osprey one hundred feet above them and the tranquil lap of water.

"You did want to be rid of her," suggested Marvell helpfully. "And she was dead already."

"I wonder," August speculated, "if it ate her. If so, I expect it might well get an upset stomach; she was very old."

August was visited by a sudden rush of guilt.

"She sacrificed herself for me," he said, glancing at Marvell. "But she was . . . inconvenient." He experienced a sense of relief, immediately followed by more guilt about feeling relief.

August was thoroughly confused about what he felt, when suddenly from the murky depths popped a dismembered arm, instantly recognizable by its unsavory, mottled hue as Claudette's.

It was followed by a violent eruption of bubbles, and the rest of Claudette.

* * *

Golden light from the setting sun illuminated the illusionists, magicians, and wizards who peopled the walls of the houseboat's cabin in posters and playbills.

"Can you please keep your arm to yourself?" wondered Marvell crossly.

She fetched the dripping limb from where it had rolled beneath a cluttered table and handed it with a grimace to Claudette.

August and Marvell watched with pained expressions as the zombie repeatedly (and unsuccessfully) attempted to restore the arm to its socket.

"She had some stitches," August explained, "up around here." He pointed to his own shoulder. "Guess it pulled away pretty easily, like overcooked chicken."

Abandoning her attempts at self-repair, Claudette cradled the dismembered arm in her other, sought out its thumb with her mouth, and began to pensively suck.

August shivered, tugging a blanket more tightly around himself, and watched as Madame Marvell placed another around the zombie's shoulders.

"I can't imagine," suggested August, "that zombies suffer much from the cold."

"It's not to keep her warm," retorted Marvell shortly, "but to keep my couch dry!"

The girl lit the burner beneath the kettle.

"Your pants should be dry by morning. You want some chicory coffee? We should warm you up."

August nodded.

"Thank you. And for saving my life, by the way."

He watched as the girl poured ground coffee into the upper container of a two-part coffeepot.

"Where," August wondered, "have you been all these months?"

"Keeping a low profile." Marvell shot August a grin. "After those child services folks got wind of me at Locust Hole, I knew I better get gone real quick."

She poured hot water from the kettle into the coffeepot.

"Round here's as good a place as any to stay invisible. It's remote, you know? Lost Souls' Swamp stretches for miles and miles all around. And there's hardly anyone that's using Channel Fifteen B—just some of those tugboats headed out for the oil rigs.

"Lucky for you it was market day at Pirates' Pier; I went in to sell some crawfish. Otherwise I'd be tucked away at the edge of the swamp somewhere."

August reached out to receive a steaming tin mug.

"I see," said Marvell, eyeing the air above August's head, "you still have your butterfly condition." She glanced at Claudette. "And your small zombie problem."

August smiled ruefully and explained that the Zombie Stone, the only means of returning Claudette to her true home, had been sold in error to an art gallery in Croissant City, and that they were on their way to recover it.

"But," observed Marvell, "you say the Malveaus left for Croissant City months ago. Seems like plenty of time for your aunt to have found that gallery and get her hands on the stone."

"Even if she has," August speculated, "it doesn't stop me from using it, right? Besides, it really belongs to the DuPonts."

"You did technically give it to her."

August shrugged.

"It hardly matters," he said glumly, "now that our canoe is somewhere down there." He cast his gaze downward, at the floor. "We have no way to travel to Croissant City."

"Of course you do," said Marvell. "I'll take you."

"You will?" August was concerned. "You're not afraid of getting caught?"

"Nah. If we keep moving and stick close to the swamp, we won't attract attention. On the Continental River near the city, there's so much water traffic and so many folks, no one would even notice us. There's just one little hitch."

August raised his eyebrows. "Hitch?"

"That monster gator bit off a chunk of the pontoon."

"But we're still afloat," observed August. "We're not sinking."

"We are afloat," admitted Marvell, "and we're not sinking. But we won't get very far. We lost an oil drum. And . . . um . . . the whole darn engine. We've got no motor. We're stranded."

CHAPTER 7

SAVE OUR SOULS

Through a scattering of butterflies, August watched the world revolve around him as the lame houseboat slowly spun. A riverbank of towering trees and dense undergrowth was followed by an arrow-straight, empty stretch of canal headed east. The other riverbank of towering trees and dense undergrowth was followed by an arrow-straight, empty stretch of canal headed west.

From a nearby wooden Adirondack chair, a crudely fashioned sackcloth doll observed August with empty button eyes. A scrap of patterned silk was pinned at its chest with a flower-shaped brooch of lilac stones.

"Can you hear that, Delfine?" wondered August. (Delfine

was named for Madame Marvell's dead grandmother.) "That's my stomach rumbling."

It had been eight hours since August was awoken by dawn light, seven since he shared the last of Marvell's sausages for breakfast. The boy thought ruefully of the package of Mudd Pies in his knapsack, now languishing in the murky depths beneath them, likely consumed by catfish and other river dwellers.

He regarded the water lapping at the barrels beneath his dangling feet, contemplating a swim to shore. But visited by the memory of yawning pink jaws, a quivering black gullet, and ice-cream-cone-sized teeth, he quickly dismissed the idea.

On further thought, he realized that, in any case, there was no shore as such to swim to—only the dense, watery undergrowth of the surrounding swamp.

He picked up Madame Marvell's binoculars from the deck, smiling as he recalled learning that the wild child, all those months ago, had been watching him, just as he had been watching her through his telescope.

He scanned the river in both directions for any sign of rescue. But the binoculars revealed nothing but a stately ibis stalking the reeds and, nearby, an abandoned "No Entry" sign languishing at a crazy angle.

August sighed. He did not relish spending a second night sleeping on the houseboat's floor.

"You know we'll hear a boat," said Marvell from the cabin doorway, "before we see it. Might as well relax. It's almost four; you know what that means!"

"Four?" August suddenly brightened; he'd almost forgotten. "Stella Starz?"

Stella Starz (in Her Own Life) was a television show surrounding the wacky exploits of a California teen and her group of loyal friends, to which August was devoted. Madame Marvell had inadvertently introduced him to Stella's world by mooring her houseboat (and her television) in sight of August's Locust Hole bedroom.

After Marvell (and her television) had departed, August had attempted to insert *Stella Starz* into the group of shows that made up the "approved" programming at Locust Hole.

But unfortunately, in the first episode to which Hydrangea had been exposed, Stella had uncovered the new school librarian as a smuggler of exotic animals—specifically, butterflies! When a flurry of the winged insects had exploded colorfully from a crate, Hydrangea had sprinted from the kitchen like an Olympian, shrieking, "Never again!"

August had desperately missed the show, particularly the camaraderie of its principal characters. Indeed, it was a desire to experience this sense of belonging for himself that had led the boy to run away with a zombie in search of a magic marble.

"But wait." August frowned. "Doesn't *Stella Starz* air on Mondays and Thursdays?"

"They repeat both episodes back to back," explained Marvell, "on Saturday afternoons."

Reception was poor in the remote forested area, and the outdated nature of the rabbit-ear antenna didn't help the situation. But despite the fuzzy picture, August felt incredibly thankful that the generator was not lost with the engine, for he was thrilled to revisit the antics of his old friend Stella and her posse.

"It's been months," he confided to Marvell with an ecstatic grin.

Perhaps it was in contrast to the empty, quiet vacuum of August's involuntary break from Stella's world, but the double episode seemed particularly jam-packed. The title character accidentally dyed her best friend Kevin's hair purple. Her other best friend Morning acquired an ill-mannered llama.

Most dramatic of all, Stella's new stepmother, Hedwig, under attack by Stella's cat, managed to stumble and horribly rip the poster of Stella's heroine Yuko Yukiyama, the one-eyed xylophonist, celebrated almost as much for her creative and glamorous eye patches as for her extraordinary percussion skills.

The situation deteriorated quickly. Accusations were made. Counter-accusations followed.

But August would have to wait to discover the fate of the

poster and of Officer Claw, for Claudette suddenly gripped his forearm. Her head was cocked. She was listening.

August turned down the volume dial on the battered old television and, sure enough, heard the distant *putt-putt-putt* of an engine.

On deck, August was greeted by the welcome sight of a small tugboat approaching from the direction of Pirates' Pier.

"Rescue!" cried the boy, stretching up his arms and waving them like scissor blades.

As the vessel drew closer, August could see a figure in the wheelhouse and another two on the bow. One of the mariners uncertainly returned August's salute.

"They think I'm just saying hello," cried August. "Wave, you guys, wave like you're in trouble!"

The tugboat was almost parallel, about to pass them in the narrow channel.

"SOS!" yelled August. "Save our souls!"

The vessel turned in their direction.

"They're coming!" cried Marvell, as Claudette joined the effort by hoisting her recovered arm high and thrashing it through the air above the children's heads.

They were moments from rescue. The vessel was only yards away, close enough now that August could see the crew's faces.

But upon the zombie's appearance, their expressions of concern were replaced by disbelief, then horror, then fear.

"No! Wait!" cried August. "She's armless . . . I mean harmless!"

But it was too late. The pilot was yanking the wheel in the opposite direction and opening up the throttle. The tugboat righted its course and made off at high speed.

"Hold tight!" cried Marvell, for the retreating vessel had churned up a powerful wake.

The houseboat flopped about violently and was swept by successive foamy ridges to the river's edge, into the reeds. As they glided past the "No Entry" sign and the startled ibis took flight, August braced himself for impact, anticipating the houseboat's collision with muddy banks and sunken tree trunks.

But as their passage remained uninterrupted and smooth, August realized that the vessel was being propelled through an inlet penetrating the stand of cypress roots, thick with water plants, but not impassable.

The sunlight sparkling on the canal retreated as, for a minute or two, the ebbing ripples of the tugboat's wake nudged the houseboat deeper into the thicket.

Just as it seemed the craft would finally become ensnared by the watery undergrowth, the leafy passage discharged the travelers into a small lagoon.

Although merely twenty yards or so from the canal, the shady pond was entirely concealed from it by densely packed trees and shrubs. The air was still and twinkled with flying insects, and the place had a lonely feeling.

But it was immediately apparent that August and his companions were not alone.

CHAPTER 8

A WATERY GRAVEYARD

At the center of the lagoon, supported on a rickety network of stilts and platforms, a ragged cluster of shacks and splintered cottages floated inches above a raft of water hyacinth.

A crudely formed jetty extended toward the houseboat, bearing a large hand-painted sign that indicated the travelers had arrived at "Gardner's Island."

Beneath the banner sat or stood several children, ranging in age from three-ish to ten-ish. All were ginger-haired and heavily freckled, and observed the drifting houseboat without expression and in complete silence.

The only movement derived from a girl, around five or six, who was swinging her legs over the water; the only sound from a mosquito buzzing in August's ear.

The crippled vessel spun slowly closer to the huts, and August's heart fluttered as he realized that the hamlet was dotted throughout with many more lurking, silent figures, motionless and ginger-haired, children and adults.

The houseboat finally came to rest against a tangle of bony forms protruding from the purple plants, which up close August realized represented a watery graveyard of corroding boat wreckage. Gazing up, the boy saw that the dwellings forming Gardner's Island were cobbled together from similar such fragments of nautical scrap, their walls and roofs formed from rudders, keels, and rust-streaked steel hull panels.

A yard away and just a foot or so higher than the houseboat's deck, the closest of the villagers—a man and a girl—squatted on the scaffold of their riveted, patched-up metal cottage, building a flat-bottomed canoe. After a moment or two of regarding the houseboat and its crew in silence, the man spoke.

"Godfrey Gardner," he said indifferently, with an almost imperceptible nod. "This my girl, Grizel. You on Gardner's Island." August looked around, confused.

"I don't see any island. This seems like the opposite of an island."

"Used to be one," said Godfrey Gardner. "Before Grizel's time." He pointed a screwdriver beyond the houseboat. "Before they sliced up the swamp with canals for their oil boats. Now when the hurricanes come, the dirt just wash away down those blasted things. Every year, less dirt, more water. Less island, more stilts. Less corn, more . . ." He waved his tool at the muddle of rusting marine salvage.

"I'm sorry, sir," said August, "about your used-to-be island." The man nodded, quietly eyeing August's butterflies and the one-armed zombie.

"You don't look like oil folks," he remarked. "What brings you down Channel Fifteen B?"

"We're headed from Pepperville to Croissant City." August glanced behind him, toward the houseboat's stern. "But we had a . . . um . . . hitch." The man studied the damaged pontoon with raised eyebrows.

"Now who, or what, you run into that might cause such a heap of trouble?"

"Would you believe me, sir, if I told you it was a giant white alligator?"

"I've heard more fantastical tales than that," Godfrey said, almost smiling, "round these parts."

Godfrey slowly scanned the entire houseboat, and August imagined he saw a look of hunger in the man's gaze. He wondered if Godfrey Gardner was mentally butchering the houseboat into sections for reuse.

"I don't suppose," August said, gazing around the uniquely composed community, "you have a spare outboard motor?"

The man stood, wiping his palms on his overalls.

"Well now," he said, "that's business talk. And round here, it's the Admiral takes care of business. You best be talking to her."

He waved his screwdriver at the children on the pier.

"Gaspard, Gilbert, Gabrielle: fetch them in and take them to the Admiral."

A rope was thrown from the jetty and, shortly thereafter, the houseboat was moored and its crew had disembarked.

Following Gaspard, Gilbert, and Gabrielle past one freckled, staring face after another, August was reminded of that certain grocer's delivery boy; the boy who had, the previous summer, been instrumental in luring August through his front door for the first time.

"Do you happen to know," he asked his young guides, "a boy named Gaston?"

"Last name Gardner?" asked Gaspard or Gilbert (August was unclear which was which).

"I'm not sure."

"Ginger hair? Freckles? Overalls?"

"Ye-es," responded August uncertainly, for this might well have described every single person in sight.

"Sure," confirmed Gaspard or Gilbert based on the scant evidence. "He's one of ours."

The orange-haired trio led the way through the water-locked village, across a confusing fretwork of creaking gangplanks and walkways.

One of these, unsettlingly long, narrow, and without bar-riers, extended into the lagoon far beyond the gently bobbing carpet of water hyacinth. Inches above the dark green water, a platform supported a unique dwelling.

The wooden bow of some antique oceangoing ship had been cleanly sawn away from the rest of the vessel and placed on end to form a sort of pointy hut. The curving, weatherworn planks of the hull were pierced by a crooked metal chimney and small windows, the latter fitted with lace curtains. What once was a horizontal hatch now served as a low-slung front door. It stood open to reveal an interior lost in shadow.

Gaspard or Gilbert disappeared inside and returned mo-mentarily.

"The Admiral awaits," he announced stiffly, as if reciting rehearsed lines.

When his eyes adjusted from brightness to gloom, August found himself in a place somewhere between an office and a junkyard. Stacked high against the walls was an impressive as-sortment of nautical salvage of the smaller variety that might fit through a front door: ships' wheels, anchors, propellers, and weathered life preservers bearing the faded names of forgotten vessels. At the center of it all presided a large desk of cream-colored metal, rust streaking from the rivets that held it together.

Much of the leather desktop was concealed by an assortment of repurposed containers, filled to brimming with even smaller treasures. A size-twelve sneaker box overflowed with leather wallets.

One large pickle jar contained rings of gold and silver, many plain, others set with gemstones. Another jar was packed with wristwatches and another with spare change.

The silence was punctuated by an occasional snapping pop that originated from the mouth of the woman behind the desk.

She was older than Hydrangea, not tall, but solidly built. Her double-chinned face was daubed with garish makeup. Sparse ginger hair peeked from beneath a bicorne hat worn side to side like those of officers and generals of the olden days. Occasional bright pink bubbles formed from her bright red lips, inflating impressively to the size of an apple before bursting with a satisfying smack.

Plastic pineapple-shaped earrings jiggled as the woman rapidly counted out paper money, rolled it into tidy wads, and secured it with rubber bands. The loose skin around her fleshy wrists jiggled too.

"Folks keep talking about some giant white gator," she said through a wad of bubble gum, without looking up. "Now they tell me it's gone and brought about some so-called hitch for you kids and your zombie pal."

August and Madame Marvell glanced at Claudette, surprised by the woman's matter-of-fact attitude.

"Round here," August remarked curiously, "you don't much

seem to mind the undead. Claudette generally causes a bit more of, um . . . a ruckus."

The Admiral swept the rolls of cash into a coffee can and raised heavy black lashes to reveal small but shrewd blue eyes.

"Sugar," she responded, working the gum like a cow chewing cud. "When you live at the edge of Lost Souls' Swamp, you see a thing or two. All manner of folks"—she stared pointedly at the lazy circle of butterflies above August's head—"pass through Gardner's Island. Mostly living. A couple not so much."

She turned her attention to Claudette as a bubble formed and popped.

"I've seen her kind before. Some call them monsters, but I say they're restless souls I do and, as such, deserving of our pity."

"Restless why?" August wondered aloud. The Admiral folded her ample arms and, chomping loudly, leaned back in her chair.

"Unfinished business I reckon. Death is rarely welcome, but when it comes, there's those of us who realize we don't belong here anymore and move along without complaint. Then there's others who are stricken before they've said what they got to say, before they've found what they got to find, before they've done what they got to do."

She wagged a finger accusingly at Claudette.

"Now, dissatisfied spirits? They can't quite quit this place. They linger somewhere nearby, not quite here, not quite there, vulnerable to those who would use some magical object—a Go-Between I reckon they call them—to reach in and drag them back."

August revealed that the trio was, in fact, on a mission to track down such a Go-Between—the one responsible for the existence of this very zombie.

"But . . . ," he explained. "Well, the alligator."

Madame Marvell nudged August pointedly and nodded at a pile of battered outboard motors leaning against an unlit iron stove.

"We were just wondering"—August cleared his throat uncomfortably—"if you might be able to help us. Ma'am. I mean, sir. I mean, Admiral."

The Admiral glanced over her shoulder to where Marvell's eyes were focused, then returned August's gaze with a look of vague amusement.

"When you live on an island, sugar," she said, "that's no longer an island, you got to make a living any ways you can. In the swamp, nothing comes for nothing. What you got in the way of exchange?"

August rummaged in his pockets and emptied them onto the desktop.

"Seventeen dollars, thirty-two cents, and an empty Mudd Pie wrapper?" scoffed the Admiral. "That'll get you one of these wallets, but one of these wallets won't get you where you want to go."

She studied August's crestfallen expression.

"I hear," she said, casually blowing and popping another bubble, "you're acquainted with our Gaston."

August nodded, thinking that Gaspard or Gilbert had certainly conveyed a generous amount of information to the Admiral during their brief conference.

"I wouldn't do this," said the Admiral, "but for a friend of the family. It's not near a fair exchange, but"—she pointed a fleshy finger—"I see something that I want."

PART II

CHAPTER 9

CROISSANT CITY

"What do you imagine," August wondered, "the Admiral wanted with Claudette's necklace? It was so old and dingy."

The boy was steering the rudder of a dented, sputtering outboard motor. As the starboard and central portion of the rear deck and transom had been lost to the alligator's jaws, the engine now sat off-center, and required constant adjustment to prevent the vessel turning in circles.

"Perhaps," speculated Marvell, "they were black pearls. Could be valuable, I reckon. At least worth a lot more than this piece of garbage." She thumbed at the coughing engine. "I hope we weren't cheated."

"I don't know," said August of the motor. "It's not that pretty, but it seems to work okay. Besides, not even black pearls could be worth more to me than getting hold of that Zombie Stone."

Marvell took the tiller as the houseboat joined a parade of larger vessels filing into Pirates' Pier Lock. The narrow channel was flanked by soaring concrete walls, and before them, August saw closed steel gates of such immensity that they might have marked the entrance to Atlantis. This impression was enhanced by the rivulets of water trickling from the joints.

The boy couldn't help but gulp, imagining the fishy world beyond, towering far above the houseboat and contained only by the man-made portal.

Equally enormous gates behind them closed, and ever so slowly, the walls appeared to grow shorter and shorter. But August understood that the craft was in fact rising on the water slowly filling the lock; a sort of elevator for boats, carrying them up and down between waterways high and low.

The great gates had also shrunk, and as a new world appeared beyond them, they finally eased open, releasing the marine traffic onto the broad brown expanse of the Continental River.

August gasped at the vastness of the uninterrupted space; he had never been anywhere so flat and open, with such a large sky unobstructed by trees and vegetation. The waterway was busy with traffic, and, despite sticking close to shore, the houseboat smacked up and down on choppy waters. Holding on tightly,

August gazed up in wonder at the passing oil tankers and seafaring vessels that literally dwarfed Marvell's ramshackle craft.

Bridges slid by overhead, impossibly long and slender. Both riverbanks were lined with wharfs and piers, vast floating banks of tethered barges, the giant gray drums and flaming chimneys of refineries, and, now and then, the creamy white columns of elegant mansions from days gone by.

The factories grew larger, the green spaces less frequent, the bridges more numerous. Eventually the tiny vessel was surrounded by warehouses, train depots, and, beyond them, the jumbled roofs of a great city.

The clouds blushed with sunset light as Marvell steered her home into the shadow of a low-slung pier where a monumental ship was moored.

This was not a liner designed to cross oceans, such as the *Queen Mary* or the *Titanic*. Rather, the vessel was of the category known as a paddleboat, designed to navigate the quieter waters of a mighty river. It was still, however, the length of a city block, a hulking great thing with four skinny black smokestacks standing side by side at either end. But the lowest of its three decks sat merely feet above the water's surface, and the entire affair was encased by delicate galleries of white wrought iron, leaving one with the impression of a giant floating summerhouse.

On the side, large letters in a font that reminded August of the circus identified the vessel as the *Delta Duchess*.

As they skirted the stern, August gazed openmouthed at the looming red paddle wheel, as enormous as might be expected to propel such a vast vessel. He was still speculating on the size of each horizontal blade (four feet deep by thirty feet wide), when Marvell killed the engine and permitted the houseboat's pontoon to gently collide with the nearby embankment formed from great boulders.

August leaped to shore, followed by Claudette, but Marvell made no move to follow.

"Aren't you coming?" inquired August. Marvell shook her head.

"Better stay with the boat," she explained. "Might get stolen or impounded by the Harbor Police. And we'll need a way out of here." She pointed to the shadowy forest of short piles supporting the pier. "Not many vessels will fit under that," she observed. "But this one will. I'll hide the boat and wait for you in there. Here, take my boatswain's whistle."

Madame Marvell showed August how to hold the gently curving brass tube to his lips and open and close his fingers over the punctured sphere at one end to produce a piercing, nautical-sounding squeal.

"I can hear that thing from half a mile away," she explained. "When you need fetching, just blow."

August nodded, pocketed the contraption, and looked up the embankment.

"I'm not sure where to go," he said. "My only map was in my knapsack, which is now at the bottom of Channel Fifteen B or possibly in a giant alligator's stomach. How will I find Aunt Orchid's house?"

"Tourist maps," explained Marvell. "They're everywhere: stacked outside restaurants, in boxes attached to lampposts." She thumbed over her shoulder. "I'm sure you'll find some up there, on the pier."

* * *

The volume of people in Croissant City made Pepperville seem positively sleepy (which of course it was, but it was the busiest place that August had ever been). It felt to the boy as if the entire population of the nation was flooding the city's streets.

The locals were also distinctly more colorful than those back in Hurricane County. In fact, it seemed that many had been invited to some giant costume party, for their clothing was, to say the least, theatrical.

Many were dressed as jesters or skeletons or angels or devils. Many others, though not identifiable as any particular character, sported eccentric accessories like feather boas or fuzzy antennae or sequined sunglasses or bizarre masks.

Almost all were heavily draped with strings of shiny beads in every color of the rainbow.

Dazed, unnerved, and overwhelmed by the festive throngs,

August clung to a lamppost with Claudette, both DuPonts jostled and bumped by the passing pedestrians. August glanced up at the street signs above them, then down at the document in his free hand, a map, entitled "Croissant City's Old Quarter."

"Looks like we're at this intersection." Releasing the post, August attempted to place his finger on the paper, but the repeated impact of clumsy passersby made this impossible. "But I'm not sure which corner. Funeral Street is way over here. I think we need to go this way. No, wait, this way."

Ushering Claudette before him, the boy attempted to cross the street in his chosen direction. But such an undertaking was like fording a torrential river, for the road was jam-packed, not with vehicles but people, all headed in the same direction.

Claudette attempted to force her way north through the east-flowing crowd. But, eventually, even the zombie's unusual strength was no match for the sheer volume of bodies, and the DuPonts found themselves helplessly swept along with the boisterous throng.

August gazed at the strange new environment surrounding him. The Old Quarter's many streets were far narrower than Pepperville's single thoroughfare. Its buildings were taller, slimmer, and more densely packed. Some were faced with exposed brick, many more with cheerfully colored stucco: yellow ochre, salmon pink, mint green.

Most sported painted wooden shutters and were fronted by an airy gallery of wrought ironwork so elaborate and delicate, it resembled black spun sugar.

Above, the balconies were festooned with bunting, flags, and tinsel of purple and gold. Below, from the ceilings of the shady arcades, dangled baskets of geraniums and ferns and numerous store signs of various shape and design. The sidewalks were peppered with obstacles in the form of fire hydrants, potted palms, and elegant lampposts with ornate bases and bulbs enclosed in old-fashioned lanterns.

From almost every direction, bursting from the open doors of numerous establishments, came the infectious, foot-tapping strains of live music in a distinctive style: a swishy, rhythmic yet unpredictable blend of trumpets, pianos, and drum brushes. The melodic, aromatic, exotic, historic place made August think of matadors and gangsters and banana trees.

And it was clearly a popular destination; the pedestrian traffic was so dense that August's feet lost contact with the ground. Wedged between solid bodies, however, the boy remained upright and in motion. He looked up at the person into whose shoulder he was pressed: a large, bald man whose face was concealed by a mask of gold braid and crimson feathers.

"Why," yelled August above the din, "are there so many people?"

"You kidding, buddy?" responded the man. "It's Carnival!" With a bellowing "Woot, woot!" he shook a bottle of champagne and removed his thumb from the neck, releasing foamy spray over the heads of those around him, who whooped with equal enthusiasm, as if being soaked by sparkling beverage was a fine thing. "Dang!" observed the man. "Where'd all these butterflies come from?"

Jammed directly in front of them, a girl whose beaded mask was crowned by silk roses was blowing through a plastic wand, producing flurries of small bubbles. Claudette's eyes swiveled with fascination and she grabbed at the soapy orbs with the outstretched fingers of her severed arm.

"Fun, huh?" said the girl. "Here, girl, have some of your own." She thrust a colorful plastic bottle at the zombie, who licked it inquisitively.

"Where is everyone going?" August asked of the champagne-wielding man.

"Dude!" The man clearly considered August a total dummy. "To the concert of cou—"

But August did not hear the end of the sentence, for he was at that moment struck forcefully from behind. Punched free from the press of bodies, he abruptly found his nose inches from the asphalt.

The boy glimpsed his map as it was swept away and shredded by a moving forest of shins. Shoe soles were smashing the ground inches from his fingers. He received a painful kick in the ribs. He struggled to rise, but knees and calves battered him from every direction. He fell again, curling up and covering his head.

"Well, this is a fine thing," he thought. "Of all the fates I imagined for myself in sleepy Locust Hole, I never imagined I'd wind up trampled to death."

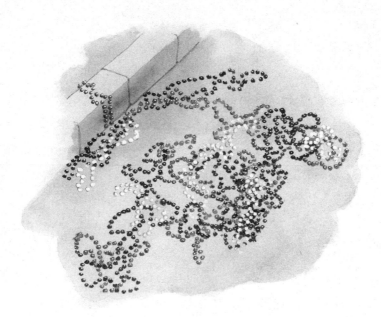

CHAPTER 10

UPON A PIRATE'S KNEE

But such an untimely end did not await our hero.

Instead, something suddenly grabbed August's jacket collar, and he was dragged forcefully upward, coming abruptly face to face with his rescuer.

Zombies, it seemed, were good for some things.

As August clung to Claudette, struggling to remain upright, he saw the buildings that rose on either side give way to a leafy canopy suspended above towering trees. He observed tall iron railings sail by, and the hard street beneath his feet gave way to a soft and spongy surface. Suddenly the press of humanity loosened up and the children found themselves deposited on a lawn. August realized that the throng, previously compressed by the narrow streets, was now dispersing into a spacious park.

Above all, towering into the dusky skies, were the three white spires of an elegant cathedral. Beneath those, August could see the tented ceiling of an event stage and the brilliant glare of spotlights mounted on a scaffold. But the shadowy, milling crowd blocked any view the children might have had of the stage itself. August heard the harsh yet muffled tones of a presenter speaking into a microphone, and when the audience suddenly roared, Claudette jumped and grunted her disapproval.

People streamed toward the attraction, revealing behind them a large public statue where the park's paths met. The looming bronze effigy, some fifteen feet high, depicted a man that to August looked vaguely familiar. He was a pirate, to be precise, who struck a swashbuckling pose, one foot planted on a banded, domed chest whose top could not quite close due to the treasure busting from within.

"Come on!" August pulled Claudette behind him. "We'll be able to see from up there." They scampered across the lawn to clamber up the statue's stepped base. As he climbed past gold lettering etched deeply into the polished granite, August read:

"Jacques LeSalt Park is named for the infamous privateer, who, at this very spot, met his end upon the gallows. Though tried and hung as a criminal, he was a folk hero to many. It is said by some that the pirate's tortured spirit still roams the local swamps, searching for a lost treasure trove of gold doubloons."

Whatever his fate, the pirate's oversized bronze knee provided the perfect perch. The spot was clearly favored by pigeons but granted August and Claudette an unobstructed view to the stage, over the sea of people.

"Most of y'all know me," the presenter was saying with enthusiastic cheer. "But for those who don't, the name is Cyril Saint-Cyr, local historian, tour guide, business owner, and general personality."

The man was rather shorter than the stand before him and gripped it with both fists, straining his neck upward to be heard through the microphone. His rosy little face, grinning from ear to ear, sat above an enormous green bow tie and was crowned by a near vertical tuft of white hair. He made August think of one of those decorative plaster garden gnomes—a garden gnome in a seersucker suit.

"And don't forget, folks," Cyril Saint-Cyr urged, waggling a rosy little finger, "that tonight's festivities are brought to you by Saint-Cyr's Wax Museum, the famous and infamous, large as life in wonderful wax! It's just around the corner. We open at nine a.m. But I won't keep you any longer, folks, because I know why y'all are here. So, come on now, let's give a big old Croissant City Carnival welcome to the one, the only . . . Yuko Yukiyama!"

Claudette managed to grab August's jacket as he nearly slid off Jacques LeSalt's pigeon-spattered pants.

"Did you hear that, Claudette?" August, eyes nearly popping out of his face, was forced to scream to be heard above the roaring crowd. "Yuko Yukiyama!" He grabbed Claudette's biceps (the one that remained attached to the rest of her) and gave her a little shake. "Yuko Yukiyama! Stella Starz's favorite musician: the one-eyed xylophonist famed almost as much for her striking eye patches as for her virtuoso talent. I can't believe it. Oh, my Lord," he cried, flattening his palm against his heart. "There she is!"

An extraordinary figure teetered onto the stage in perilously high platform boots, eliciting a deafening, ecstatic welcome from the audience.

Yuko Yukiyama had electric-blue hair, wound tightly into conical knots that protruded from her skull like pointy horns. She wore a very high-collared gown, constructed from what appeared to be Bubble Wrap, and a brilliantly sparkling heart-shaped eye patch of candy-pink sequins. The musician turned in circles, her arms akimbo. From each fist extended a slender stick topped by a ball tightly wound with thin yarn.

"Those," August informed Claudette, "are called mallets. I know, because Stella Starz says that Yuko Yukiyama creates more magic with her mallets than a wizard does with his wand."

Cyril Saint-Cyr was meanwhile pressing his palms downward, attempting to quiet the howling crowd.

"I know! I know y'all are more riled up than hornets in a

soccer ball," he cried as the roaring petered out. "But just wait, folks, till y'all hear this. For one very special performance, Yuko will require"—he paused for dramatic effect—"a volunteer!" Another roar accompanied an instant forest of hands stretching desperately into the air.

Saint-Cyr smiled impishly. "But, given that there are so many of y'all, this very special honor will be awarded"—he peered around with a palm leveled above his eyebrows—"to the fan who has put the most effort into their costume tonight."

The event host turned and swished his hand at some invisible party in the scaffolding. From there, a blinding spotlight popped on and proceeded to scan the hysterical audience, briefly highlighting all the jesters and skeletons, angels and devils, and numerous nightmarish masks sprouting beaks or antlers or feathers.

The brilliant, bluish circle of light swept swiftly across the statue of Jacques LeSalt, paused, then abruptly jerked back.

There, it stopped decisively, dramatically illuminating a ragged, startled figure perched on the statue's knee: Claudette DuPont.

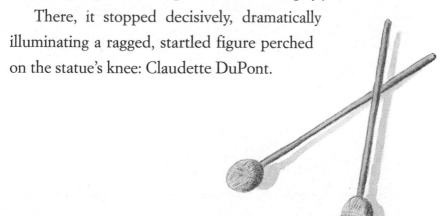

CHAPTER 11

A SYMPHONY FOR SKULLS
IN G MINOR

August pushed and shoved his way past heavy, closely packed bodies and began to weary of this obstructive—unhelpful even—crowd.

He jumped frequently, grabbing shoulders to gain more height, desperately trying to keep sight of Claudette, who was being passed, literally like a rag doll, across the audience and toward the stage.

August wondered if his undead great-great-aunt was in fact enjoying the whole thing, for a goofy grin was plastered across her pasty face as it bobbed about.

On the rickety steps to the podium, the boy tripped over something soft but solid and was not entirely surprised, given the physical commotion, to find himself retrieving Claudette's severed arm. He was scrambling with it onto the stage, just as Saint-Cyr ushered Claudette to the microphone and asked her name.

"It's Claudette," gasped August, stumbling forward and speaking so closely into the mic that he caused a cringeworthy screech of feedback. "She doesn't speak English; she's from . . ." He paused, wincing at what he was about to say. "Lapland."

The boy shook his head just a little, recalling the previous terrible conclusion to this old lie; surely, second time around, it was even more transparent.

"Well, we congratulate this young Arctic person," gushed Cyril Saint-Cyr, who appeared entirely unsuspicious of August's explanation or of Claudette's origin, "on such dedication to her Carnival costume. So realistic. So deliciously unpleasant. The dismembered limb." He flapped his hands at the arm cradled in August's own. "Very clever. However do you do it? And you, young man, with the butterflies. Are they battery operated? A hologram? Whatever the case, it's a nifty trick. Now tell us, are you two in some way related?"

"Um. Well. Actually, sir," August explained, "I'm her great-great-nephew."

"Well, isn't that just darling?" suggested Saint-Cyr. "Families can be so darn complicated these days. Can't they?"

The presenter guided Claudette by the hand ("Why, child, you're cold as a snowman's hug; you should consider some gloves like your great-great-nephew's") to center stage, where Yuko awaited behind a curious instrument: a slender console that supported a row of colored plastic skulls. The one-eyed percussionist bowed very deeply to Claudette and offered her a mallet. Claudette stared at the thing, a tiny strand of drool dangling from her blue lips.

"Take it!" hissed August. Glancing nervously in his direction, Claudette obeyed.

Yuko faced the instrument, her own mallet raised. A deeply expectant hush fell across Jacques LeSalt Park.

After several increasingly agitating moments of silence, a bulb within one of the plastic skulls lit up. Yuko struck it, and a note, clear and true, reverberated through the giant speakers, filling everything around with its exquisite sound. The audience responded with a rapturous sigh. Another skull lit up. Another clear, exquisite note followed. Another skull, another note. The formula became clear.

When a turquoise-colored skull lit up immediately in front of Claudette, Yuko withheld her mallet, but nodded pointedly at the zombie. Claudette hesitated, eyes swiveling.

"Hit it!" August hissed again, batting the zombie with her own arm. She did, producing another perfect note. The crowd cheered. Claudette beamed.

And so the performance continued, and a melody began to emerge. Claudette, although jerky and inelegant, grew more

confident and adept. When she struck an illuminated skull before even Yuko could reach it, the xylophonist and the audience
were delighted. The tempo accelerated, and a true duet ensued.
The percussionist began to show off, twirling her mallet in the
air and even around her back between notes.

August noticed a greedy look in Claudette's eye when she
observed the swell in audience appreciation for Yuko's antics.
Without warning, the zombie tossed her own mallet into the
air, snatched her severed arm from August, and, with its hand,
caught the descending mallet.

"Oh, bravo! Bravo!" cried Saint-Cyr, clapping like a child as
the crowd went nuts. "Now that's what I call a costume!"

With the extension provided by her severed limb, Claudette
could reach the far ends of the instrument, and she and Yuko
artfully interwove across the keyboard, producing a frantic,
breathtaking performance of such beauty that there was not a
dry eye in the audience.

When the skulls finally went dark, there was a full five minutes of deafening applause.

Saint-Cyr was growing hoarse before he could finally calm
the crowd.

"I think we can all agree," he pronounced, "that we have
seen percussion history made here tonight." The man faced
Claudette. "I'm delighted to tell you that for being such a good
sport, and such a terrifying zombie"—he turned to the audience

and winked theatrically—"that you are to receive two tickets—not one, but two—donated by the Guild of Weepy Widows, to ride on their annual float in Tuesday's Carnival Grand Parade.

"But wait, there's more," he said, and held up a palm to quiet the cheers. "These very special ticket holders will be lucky enough to share the float with the parade's celebrity grand marshal.

"And, this year, that esteemed post will be filled by TV teen sensation Stella Starz's . . . cat, Officer Claw!"

CHAPTER 12

THE HOUSE OF ZOMBIES

Two able stagehands strong-armed August and Claudette toward an opening in the black fabric backdrop as a group of musicians carrying instruments (August noticed a French horn, a saxophone, and an accordion) hurried past them toward the stage.

Behind them, Cyril Saint-Cyr was making another introduction. "While Miz Yukiyama," he was saying, "changes costume yet *again,* please welcome Croissant City's very own Papa Jax and the Jazzy Razzmatazz Cats!"

The DuPonts stumbled down some scaffold steps into a hive of activity on the grass behind the stage. Lighting technicians, makeup artists, and performers bustled about, featureless silhouettes against the luminous white stucco of the cathedral.

August nudged Claudette and nodded toward a nearby exchange between Yuko Yukiyama and a thin, limp young man in a plaid suit. The latter was presenting a wooden case with one hand and, with the other, holding open its lid. Inside was a kaleidoscope of sparkling, glamorous eye patches.

Although she was speaking in another language (August assumed Japanese), he could tell by her tone and volume that Yuko was not happy. "No," the panicked young man was protesting, "I haven't seen the black crystal one. You wore it in Paris. Perhaps you left it . . ." But the discussion was promptly concluded when Yuko bonked the poor fellow on the head with her fuzzy-balled mallet and stormed off in a rustle of Bubble Wrap.

"Theatrical types!" declared Cyril Saint-Cyr, popping up from nowhere. "They can be so temperamental, don't you find? I can assure you, that is not the first noggin to be bopped by a Yukiyama mallet. Oh, my Lord." He swatted aside a butterfly. "They're almost like the real thing. So clever! Now, you young people wait right here while I fetch your release forms."

August, suddenly dazed and overwhelmed by the whirlwind of events, took a seat on an unplugged subwoofer.

"I can scarcely believe it," he muttered, half to Claudette, half to himself. "I am actually going to meet Officer Claw. *The* Officer Claw, the cat that shares a pillow, and sometimes tuna sushi, with Stella Starz! I might pet the same patchy fur that Stella has petted."

August studied the zombie's vacant expression.

"I know what you're thinking, Claudette: Claw is an unusual choice for Carnival grand marshal. Any cat would be, I reckon. But I promise you, if any cat can do it, this cat can.

"Officer Claw is an exceptionally clever animal. He can understand three languages. He can play 'Stray Cat Strut' on a regular-sized piano. He is even a master of disguise, although, admittedly, he mainly impersonates other cats. Stella Starz describes him as a shining example to feline-kind across the universe." August kicked his heels against the subwoofer.

"Do you think Officer Claw will wear a costume on the float? He would look very impressive, I think, in a superhero outfit."

August was picturing Officer Claw with a rainbow mohawk when Saint-Cyr returned wearing red spectacles that seemed far too large for his head and clutching some forms.

"Now, sign right here." He placed the forms next to August on the subwoofer. "Just so. And here. And here. Oh, and here. Now, the young lady." Claudette received the pen in the hand of her dismembered arm and Cyril guffawed with delight. "Most remarkable. Quite the best costume. My, that is a very large signature. Maybe keep it on the paper? Oh, not quite so hard, young lady, you're ripping it."

Saint-Cyr set aside the forms and unfolded a fresh document.

"Just a few little instructions," he assured them, "for the day of. Keep things smooth sailing, yes?" He adjusted his oversized glasses and, keeping place with his finger, read: " 'One. Kindly address the grand marshal as Mr. Claw. Two. Avoid the topics of dogs and llamas; Mr. Claw does not care for either. Three. Absolutely and positively no sudden movements within the grand marshal's vicinity.' "

August nodded sagely, recalling that the incident leading to the destruction of Yuko Yukiyama's poster was provoked by Hedwig's abrupt and unannounced entrance into Stella's room.

" 'Riders must be in place,' " Saint-Cyr continued, " 'thirty minutes before the parade begins.' " He lowered the instruction sheet and addressed the children directly. "The staging area is just north of River and Dolphin. Where are y'all staying?"

August pulled a scrap of paper from his pocket.

"I wrote it down so I wouldn't forget it. It's 591 Funeral Street, sir. Can you tell us how to get there? I lost my map. Why, whatever is the matter, Mr. Saint-Cyr?"

"You are guests in"—Saint-Cyr's eyes were bulging—"in . . . the House of Zombies?"

"The . . . what?" August's eyes slid toward Claudette.

Cyril leaned in, glancing around with a mischievous glimmer in his eyes, as if about to divulge juicy gossip.

"Many houses in this city," he said in a hushed tone, "have strange and even bloody histories. Gruesome murders. Disturbing hauntings. But perhaps none has a past more macabre

than that of 591 Funeral Street, once home to the necromancer
Orfeo DuPont. Have you heard of him?"

August nodded, desperately attempting to appear unlike
anyone that might be related to the gentleman in question.

"Then you'll have learned, no doubt, of his infamous act at
the Theatre Français (which, incidentally, is now home to Saint-
Cyr's Wax Museum: the famous and infamous, large as life in
wonderful wax!)."

Saint-Cyr's rosy, gnomish little face took on a devilish glee as
he continued.

"DuPont's Dance of the Dead was a ghoulish form of en-
tertainment in which the magician employed a so-called
Go-Between—the Zombie Stone he called it, if I remember
correctly—to compel the dead to perform a grotesque ballet.

"Well, his house is immediately behind the theater. The Old
Quarter, after all, was built long before anyone had thought of
suburbs; butchers and confectioners, offices and homes are all
jumbled together in the tight and crowded streets. It is not un-
common for a smart dwelling to share a wall with a café, or a toy
store, or . . . some other commercial building.

"Legend has it, in fact, that DuPont built a secret passage to
discreetly move his undead performers between the house and
the theater.

"Ever since DuPont's Dance of the Dead closed and the
theater fell into darkness and disrepair, there have been reports

of strange noises at night—crashes and strangled groaning—emitting from the so-called Zombie House next door. Some claim to have seen eerie, crooked figures lurching past the windows.

"Even the DuPont family eventually abandoned the place; I can't imagine why a genteel lady such as Orchid Malveau might have bought it."

"Are you suggesting," August wondered, "that the house is haunted?"

"Some might say so," said Saint-Cyr coyly. "No one knows for sure. But I can tell you this much." The little, mischievous, rosy face came in close.

"After Orfeo DuPont left town, no one ever found those zombies."

CHAPTER 13

THE GUILD OF WEEPY WIDOWS

August and Claudette proceeded through a quieter corner of
the Old Quarter.

The streets here were narrow and hushed compared to
the hectic avenues closer to the river. The buildings were still
elegant, but more modest, and frequently punctuated by walled
gardens. Occasional Carnival revelers passed in pairs and small
groups, subdued and staggering, draped in the swishing strands
of brightly colored beads.

Night had fallen completely by the time the DuPonts spied a
large, windowless mass at the corner of a sleepy junction.

"That must be the side wall of the Theatre Français," said
August quietly, turning onto Funeral Street. They proceeded,
keeping close to the magnolia trees that lined the curb. Shortly,

beside a brick wall, in the deep shadows cast by a palm tree spreading from within, August stopped.

"That's it, 591," said the boy, pointing to the structure on the opposite side of the street.

The house was grander than most, but typical of the Old Quarter style, with lofty French windows and an ornate iron gallery supported on impossibly slender posts. Beneath the balcony on the right, where house met theater, was a wide double wooden gate. Through the gap above it, August could detect a wide passage that ran beneath the upper floor of the house and into some leafy darkness beyond. Beneath the balcony on the left, two stone steps led to the front door.

The upper windows were shuttered and, indeed, the entire place was in total darkness, appearing to be without life. August was reminded of his first arrival at Château Malveau. Like her grand country mansion, Orchid Malveau's townhouse was shrouded in a thick air of gloom; sadness, even.

But suddenly a lively burst of golden light appeared at one of the lower windows. A drapery was drawn back partly to reveal a perfect, symmetrical, and very familiar face: that of a honey-haired boy, only slightly older than August himself. Beauregard Malveau, August's cousin, peered up and then down the street, and August shrank behind the overhanging palm fronds, experiencing an unpleasant rush of apprehension.

August knew that despite his angelic appearance, Beauregard was no angel. "What will he say," wondered August, "when he sees me? How mean will he be? What should I say? How are you supposed to greet someone who has betrayed you and said how much they dislike you . . . in public?" August suddenly felt nauseous. He looked back down the street, to the safe anonymity of the Old Quarter.

"If I didn't need that Zombie Stone so badly . . ."

Beauregard spun around, as if unexpectedly assaulted, and his friend Langley appeared behind him, laughing and wielding a fencing saber. Beauregard lunged at the lanky boy, who leaped backward, saber held high. Beauregard had Langley's wrist, but the tussle ceased abruptly, and the boys, suddenly subdued, turned to face the same direction.

A figure, draped entirely by a glittering veil, moved into view, carrying something black and shapeless.

"There's Aunt Orchid," whispered August. Orchid Malveau waved her free hand about, clearly delivering some instructions, and the boys disappeared, then reappeared, apparently moving a table into the center of the room. They were assisted by a third set of hands. August could not see their owner's face, but, judging by the freckles on the forearms, he guessed they belonged to Gaston, the third member of Beauregard's trio. "Gaston Gardner," muttered August, and for some reason, the full name made him smile.

With a sweeping motion, Orchid unfurled the black lace cloth in her arms and covered the table. She pointed. The lights dimmed. The walls suddenly danced with the flicker of candlelight.

Orchid noticed the open drape, gestured, and abruptly all returned to darkness.

"Come on," sighed August heavily. "We better get this over with now. It looks like they're getting ready for dinner. I wouldn't want to disturb them while they're eating."

On the front steps, August paused to study a cast-iron plaque attached to the wall beside the front door. " 'Old Quarter Historical Monument Number Seventeen,' " he read. " 'The House of Zombies.' " Below, there was a shortened version of the tale recently communicated to the DuPonts by Cyril Saint-Cyr.

"Well, if it didn't deserve the name before"—August glanced at the small zombie beside him—"it's about to!"

August placed his hand on the heavy gold door knocker. It was fashioned in the shape of a capital "M." "M" for "Malveau." "M" for "magnificence." "M" for "malevolence."

But the knocker remained still.

All the horror and shame the boy had suffered at the hands of his wealthy relatives came flooding back. He could still hear their words: "Zombie lover." "The ghost of Locust Hole." "You have failed." August shook his head.

"I . . . I can't do it, Claudette. I can't face these people again."

He turned to leave.

Claudette grabbed his arm.

"No! No, I'm sorry," August insisted, pulling sharply away and stumbling into the street, where he collided with a rapidly approaching woman, who in turn caused a pileup of the pedestrians immediately in her wake.

Luckily for everyone involved, the woman was of a stout and solid frame, and quite unruffled by the multiple collisions.

August stammered his apologies.

"Oh, come now, child." The woman, settling her chin into her chest, smiled sympathetically. "Don't you give it a second thought. I know just where you're at; grief can leave us blinder than a raccoon in a top hat."

"Um . . . I . . . grief?" August was puzzled.

"Sorrow, melancholy." The woman pulled the corners of her mouth down. "Whatever you care to call it. You are here for the event, obviously, judging by the tragedy in your little faces. There, there, child." She dabbed her handkerchief at the corners of August's eyes. "Fret not, Champagne Fontaine is here."

Champagne Fontaine wore a tiny beribboned hat upon her perfectly styled pink-gray hair and carried a large purse. Her thick wrists ended in tiny hands, and her thick ankles in tiny high-heeled shoes. She was dressed entirely in black, as were all her companions.

The funereal assembly peered at August and Claudette over Champagne's shoulder, through black veils, and from under the black brims of elaborate black hats and bonnets. Most pressed handkerchiefs to their irritated red noses, sniffling miserably.

"There are," muttered Champagne, swatting at an intrusive butterfly, "an unusual quantity of bugs at large this evening, don't you find? Now, tell me, my dears. Is this your first séance? They can seem a little creepy to begin with, I imagine. But we, the Guild of Weepy Widows"—she gestured at the entourage behind her—"find it most agreeable to converse with our dearly departed. I've had the most animated conversations with my dearest Henri. Oh, no need for tears, sugar."

August, completely dry-eyed, made a baffled expression.

"It won't be all withered ancients like us," Champagne assured him. "There will be other young people present."

The lady made for the step, taking Claudette's hand, oblivious to the fact that it belonged to a dismembered arm.

"My grandson Langley and his friend Gaston are here, guests, you understand, of the young Mister Beauregard. Such fine folks the Malveaus, are they not? I am beyond delighted that Mister Beau has taken our Langley under his wing. So reassuring to know he's mixing with the right sort."

She gave the knocker a hearty rap, smacked aside a butterfly, and fished for something in her purse.

"Do you have your card ready, child? All, I say *all* the best people leave their calling cards on the entry table."

August was trying to explain that he was only twelve years old and never called on anyone, when the door opened, and he and Claudette were swept helplessly by the Guild of Weepy Widows into the House of Zombies.

CHAPTER 14

THE ORACULUM NEVER LIES

Attendees had been filling the Malveaus' salon for several minutes now, and the DuPont children, pressed against heavy satin draperies by the windows, had become increasingly concealed behind the swelling crush of sniffling, weepy people.

The only indication of their presence was a solitary butterfly perched contentedly on August's dented helmet. August was forced to crane his neck to get a glimpse of the room beyond the many black-clad backs and shoulders stacked in front of him.

The house at 591 Funeral Street, being a city dwelling, was obviously smaller than Château Malveau, but was every bit as opulent. Important-looking artwork adorned the walls. Plush rugs were soft underfoot. Greek heroes carved from creamy marble were poised on slender stands. The ornate moldings flickered with the scattered shadows thrown by candlelight. Gleaming mahogany furniture had been stacked in the corners to accommodate the visitors and to leave a space for the circular table with four chairs at the center of the room.

One of these chairs was occupied by Orchid Malveau, who wore a long-suffering expression as Champagne Fontaine, who sat beside her, gushed enthusiastically.

"You are an invaluable addition to the guild, Orchid!" Champagne clutched Orchid's wrist. "The most miserable of us all, the jewel in our crown. We can't thank you enough for hosting tonight, and in"—she fluttered her tiny, gloved hand through the air—"such splendid circumstances."

A third chair held a thin-nosed man in a silk top hat, who repeatedly checked his pocket watch. The fourth chair remained empty.

Directly opposite, through a peephole in the crowd, August could see Beauregard lounging carelessly against a column. Langley's face popped briefly into view as he nudged August's cousin. The friends glanced in the same direction. Beauregard smiled in a mean-spirited way, clearly in response to Langley's comment. Langley smothered silent laughter. The pair appeared to be amusing themselves at someone else's expense.

"At least," thought August, "it's not mine."

The salon was now filled to capacity and buzzed with whispers and fidgeting and a general air of electric anticipation.

"Have you heard who is coming?"

"Is it true? Champagne says he's the very best!"

"Ow!" whispered August resentfully as one of the weepy widows stepped on his foot.

With a frosty smile, Orchid removed Champagne's hand from her wrist and stood.

"Ladies," she said, then a little louder, to attract their attention. "Ladies! And of course"—she nodded at the thin-nosed man—"gentleman. My fellow members of the Guild of Weepy Widows." She swept her palmetto fan around the gathering. "I know you are all excited to meet our special guest tonight, of whom our dear friend Champagne Fontaine speaks so highly. You are no doubt anxious to communicate with your loved ones on the other side, but I must ask you to exercise patience and decorum and permit the readings to proceed in an orderly fashion."

There was a sudden and decisive rap at the front door, and the assembly went deathly silent.

"It's him!" a woman in front of August whispered excitedly into the ear of another.

Orchid looked expectantly toward the foyer.

"Is that the gentleman, Escargot?"

August caught a glimpse of Escargot, the Malveau's toad-like butler, near the front door. Orchid nodded at his inaudible response.

"All right, then," Orchid declared. "Friends, please make way for esteemed medium and clairvoyant, Professor Tiberius Leech!"

Bodies parted to create a path, and from it emerged a man in a thin tie and rumpled linen suit, who paid little heed to the wide-eyed, breathless congregation.

Professor Tiberius Leech was of an indeterminate age, somewhere, August figured, between thirty and sixty years old. Bulbous, pug-like eyes filled the lenses of thick black spectacles perched on a face that had the soft, round quality of a baby's and shone with a misting of perspiration.

Both fists were held before his chest, gripping the iron handle of an exotic-looking drum-shaped box. Its leather casing was tooled with sinister symbols and was so ancient that in places it had flaked away to reveal the wood beneath.

"Why, Professor Leech, how delightful that we should meet again," prattled Champagne Fontaine in hushed tones, stretching over to awkwardly pat his arm as he placed himself beside the table before the vacant chair. "You honor us indeed with your presence. The Guild of . . ."

She was interrupted by a sharp smack from Orchid's fan.

"On behalf," Orchid said sharply, throwing Champagne a look, "of the Guild of Weepy Widows, I welcome you to my home."

"Hmm." An apparently unimpressed Professor Leech

glanced briefly at Orchid with a polite smile, while drawing gray gloves onto his hands and flexing his fingers.

He unlatched and opened the box, revealing an interior lined with crimson satin, which, unlike the exterior, looked new and pristine. From inside the lid, Professor Leech drew a circular plinth of dark, polished wood and placed it upon the table.

Both hands slid into the main compartment of the box.

"The Oraculum," announced Professor Leech, "is as old as history itself." His voice was not loud, but such was the breathless stillness of the room, it filled the space. "The Oraculum has seen empires rise from dirt and fall back into the ocean." His elbows were moving upward as he lifted something—something with some heft—from the box. "The Oraculum never lies."

There was an audible collective gasp as the crystal ball appeared. It was about the size of a small watermelon, but perfectly, perfectly spherical, and of a glass so lustrous and clear, it was mesmerizing. Sparkling candlelight revealed its surface, but its center seemed endless, impossible to define.

Gazing into its depths, August felt a dizziness akin to vertigo. He became aware of a faint whispering, very close to his right ear. But he was wedged against the wall; there was no one behind him.

It was joined by a second whisper. And a third.

August looked around, but everyone near him stood engrossed, in spellbound silence. The boy was reminded of a day long ago, when he ventured into an overgrown cemetery and heard a voice that was difficult to place, that seemed almost to originate from inside himself.

With the ball cradled in its stand and the box deposited on the floor, the professor sat, removed his gloves, and pushed his glasses up his nose. He bowed his head and placed his naked palms inches from the orb on either side.

August felt a sudden surge of energy from the table, like the shockwaves of a small explosion, and he was physically forced backward into the draperies and the window behind them.

The professor frowned, paused, then darted a quick, suspicious look around the room.

"The spirits are close tonight," he said, almost accusingly. "Very close. Someone here has an unusually strong connection to the dead."

"Oh," Champagne laughed, "it's probably me. My Henri and I were so very devoted, as you know, Professor. Is he here? Will he finally divulge the secret ingredient of his mother's gumbo recipe? I know you've asked him before, Professor, but do ask again!"

"Enough!" Orchid slapped her fan on the table and a startled Champagne was immediately silenced. "Professor Leech"— Orchid recovered her composure and genteel manner—"is here as my guest . . . at my expense." She was now, pointedly, addressing the professor. "Professor Leech will make time for all"—Orchid glanced around with a small smile—"after he has attended to *my* reading."

The professor was left in no doubt as to who was in charge here. He nodded and resumed his position, and again August felt a rising swell of something he could not explain: a great presence of . . . of what? He was not sure.

Whisper, whisper.

A hundred whispers.

August's head swam.

"The Oraculum," said Leech, glancing up at Orchid, "perceives that you are in search of something. Something of enormous importance to you."

The rings on her fingers glinted as Orchid clenched her fists and raised her chin defiantly. But she remained silent.

"You care," continued Leech, darkly, "about nothing else. Nothing."

"Can you . . ." Orchid's voice was thick and she faltered. She cleared her throat. "Can you locate this thing? Can you show me where it is?"

Leech bowed his head farther. His hands began to shake. Moisture upon his brow gathered into beads of sweat. He muttered something impossible to decipher.

August's knees grew weak. The whispers increased in number and volume to a deafening babble. August grabbed the fabric of the draperies behind him, afraid that he might faint.

The audience suddenly reacted. There were numerous gasps and small cries.

Vapors had suddenly appeared, swirling in the crystal ball.

"What is that?"

"There's something there!"

Leech was trembling all over. His eyes bulged. The miasma began to collect into something more solid, a shape. Orchid leaned in, her wild stare reflecting the light. There was a look of manic greed in her expression.

"It's a head," cried the sharp-nosed, top-hatted man. "No, a face."

"Well, bless my soul," cried Champagne Fontaine. "I am acquainted with that tragic little face. Now, that is the young man I encountered on the step outside this very house tonight.

"That boy . . . is standing right over there!"

CHAPTER 15

THE CHAMBER OF MUSIC

"What, dear nephew," said Orchid with a smile, sweet yet frosty like strawberry ice cream, "are you doing here?"

"Yeah!" agreed Beauregard less sweetly.

The DuPonts and Malveaus were gathered in the chamber of music. At least, this is how the room had been styled by Escargot the butler as he had bustled August and Claudette into it. The only visible instrument, however, was an enormous gilded harp rising before a tall mirror.

The space seemed, in fact, to act more as an annex of Orchid's gemstone collection, which August had first encountered at the Malveaus' mansion, near Pepperville. Every available surface was populated by glass cloches displaying colorful rocks.

August speculated that these perhaps represented the most

valuable of his aunt's specimens, for unlike the selection at Château Malveau, none were dull or unremarkable. All sparkled intensely with clear and vivid hues: deep ocean blue, bright grass green, sunny primrose yellow. He wondered if a brilliantly scarlet, many-faceted stone the size of a chicken's egg could possibly be a ruby.

The chamber of music was in reality an extension of the salon, the transition between the two marked by four square fluted pillars. In the front room, the weepy widows remained largely absorbed by Leech's readings, but from the corner of his eye, August was aware of an occasional curious face twisting around to observe the family drama unfolding behind them.

"How, dear nephew," continued Orchid, "did you even arrive at this place?" She paused with a sudden thought. "That nitwit . . . rather, my sister Hydrangea has not accompanied you . . . has she?"

August shook his head.

"I left her a note so she wouldn't worry," he explained. "And mostly, we rowed here. Well, Claudette did." Claudette grinned sheepishly, waggling her dismembered arm from side to side.

Orchid's smile was not really a smile.

August noticed that over his aunt's shoulder was a second Orchid.

Looming above the fireplace was a grandly framed oil painting, a Malveau family portrait. August concluded that it must have been painted several years ago, as Beauregard and his twin sister, Belladonna, were clearly much younger, maybe five or so years old.

At the rear stood a handsome man, which August assumed was Orchid's late husband, holding the young Belladonna in his arms. Beauregard leaned against the arm of a chair, in which lounged a woman instantly recognizable as August's aunt.

But the painted Orchid provided a stark contrast to the living one. She wore a breezy floral dress and was arranged in a carefree pose, one hand limply draped, holding her fan, the other resting on Beauregard's arm.

August marveled at how relaxed and happy the family looked and was struck by the realization that they must have suffered greatly to arrive at their present mournful state. But his brow creased. There was something about the painting that felt a little off. Something that felt contradictory. But before he could consider the matter further, his attention was again demanded by his immediate circumstances.

"You and your filthy DuPont zombie," growled Beauregard, "are not welcome here."

August glanced at his cousin nervously but addressed his aunt.

"You haven't found it yet, have you? Orfeo's Cadaverite, the Zombie Stone. That's what you wanted Professor Leech to locate for you."

Orchid regarded her nephew with pursed lips.

"I have not," she confirmed reluctantly. "Belladonna stubbornly refuses to remember the name of the gallery that acquired it. I've had the children, Escargot, even private detectives scour the city, but of gallery or stone, no one has found any sign. Now the twins are busy with school, fencing lessons. Escargot has no neck to speak of . . ." Orchid trailed off with a vague flap of her fan.

August failed to see the significance of Escargot's anatomy but recognized an opportunity.

"We could help you look, ma'am," he suggested quietly.

Orchid sighed with strained composure.

"If paid professionals have failed in the task, what could two bedraggled children, one of them, by the way, quite dead, possibly hope to achieve?"

"What harm could it do?" August gently pushed back. "I'm not in school. Claudette has nothing but time."

Orchid observed the zombie. August could see her begin to consider the suggestion. He was suddenly aware of his aunt's distinctive perfume. Gardenias. The lady tilted her head; calculation showed in her expression.

"You," said Orchid, curious. "I recognize you. From that old photograph in the parlor of Locust Hole."

"She's your great-aunt," explained August. "Claudette DuPont."

Orchid nodded, deep in thought.

"Who would credit it?" she muttered, more to herself than anyone present. "A relative of mine, risen clear up from the dead. How . . . unexpected. If there was ever anyone"—she paused, thinking—"qualified to find the Zombie Stone, I suppose it would be a zombie."

She decided.

"Very well."

"What?" cried Beauregard so loudly that he drew glances from several weepy widows.

"You and this . . . Aunt Claudette"—Orchid flapped at the zombie—"may stay here. Perhaps, August, you might redeem yourself after your last, let's say, misadventure."

August felt small when reminded of his previous failure to acquire the Zombie Stone for his aunt. He did not especially like Orchid. He certainly did not trust her; her interest in the Cadaverite, rare as it might have been, seemed excessive for an amateur collector of minerals.

Hydrangea had assured August that her sister was motivated by greed, or bitterness deriving from a family feud. Perhaps both. But August recognized desperation in his aunt's obsession.

He recognized it because it rivaled his own.

"There is something," August thought, "that Aunt Orchid is not revealing."

"But, Mama!" Beauregard was horrified by his mother's

invitation. "The butterflies! The zombie! It's violent; it pushed me! In front of everyone! I was humiliated!"

Without looking at him, Orchid pointed her fan at her son.

"Had you and your sister located the thing," she said coldly, "this conversation would hardly be necessary. Stop whining and go play with your little sword. Escargot! For the time being, it seems the DuPonts will be our guests; ensure my nephew gets a set of house keys."

Beauregard's face darkened with fury.

"Your luggage?" Orchid inquired of August.

"Our boat sank, ma'am."

Orchid rolled her eyes.

"That sounds about right," she said. "And some pajamas, Escargot. And tooth-brushes." She briefly studied Claudette. "Well, one toothbrush. Now, let me see. With Beauregard's friends here, all of the bedrooms are occupied tonight." Orchid flapped her fan toward the rear windows flanking the harp.

"Kindly settle my nephew and great-aunt in the carriage house. And, August, let's try keeping the butterflies to a minimum, hmm?"

CHAPTER 16

RECRUITED AND PERFECTED

Escargot, arms laden with bedding, wore an expression that suggested he was about as thrilled by the DuPonts' arrival as Beauregard.

Ushered through a back door, August found himself in a compact subtropical oasis contained within the courtyard behind the house. Gravel paths wound past planters crowded with lush, flowering plants. Mossy stone cupids peeked through leaves the size of serving platters. The fronds of towering palm trees swished overhead. At the courtyard's center lay a low-walled pond, where exotic black-specked fish lurked beneath lily pads.

On the left, a narrow wing of the house flanked the closed space. On the right loomed a tall brick wall, sooty stains and numerous patches marking its age. High above, painted letters faded to shadows read "Theatre Français."

Facing August, at the far side of the courtyard, sat an outbuilding with a large pair of doors, like those of an old-fashioned garage. Nestled beneath the structure's roof was a low-slung second floor with small darkened windows.

Escargot yanked open an obstinate second—pedestrian—door and August entered a gloomy space largely filled by a decrepit automobile from a bygone age, with thin, spindly-spoked wheels, lantern-shaped headlights, and a general appearance more reminiscent of horse-drawn buggies than a modern car. The entire vehicle was the color of rust, and its canvas roof hung in shreds.

Escargot squeezed past it toward a narrow wooden staircase and called up, "Miz Belladonna?"

August was suddenly assailed by the acrid, familiar smell of lacquer. It transported him to the moment he first met Belladonna crafting her pasta jewelry in the grotto-like gloom of Château Malveau's salon.

"Escargot? What are you doing out here?"

August recognized his cousin's voice. Although they had parted on amicable terms, he was still a little intimidated by the prickly young lady.

"We have"—Escargot paused, casting a disdainful glance at the DuPonts—"unexpected guests!"

The upper floor reminded August of his garret bedroom at Locust Hole, for it was jam-packed with towers of storage boxes and long-ago things retired from daily use: a pitchfork, a Chinese parasol, a rocking horse with three legs.

In a clearing at the center, behind a tableful of bottles and packages of pasta, sat Belladonna. An elaborate necklace of black-lacquered fusilli hung about her neck. She was hunkered over, occupied with varnishing a sheet of lasagna, when a single butterfly alighted on the table before her. Her head snapped up.

"August?" Her eyes opened wide. "What on earth? Oh, and your zombie too? Good Lord, what happened to her arm?"

"Alligator," explained August. "We're here to—oh!"

August quickly grasped the bundle that Escargot had roughly thrust against his chest.

"I've included an old pair of pajamas for the gentleman, and a nightgown for the young . . . well, *that*."

August mumbled his thanks.

"The pleasure, sir, is all mine," responded Escargot (although it clearly wasn't) as he retreated down the creaking stairs.

August shared with Belladonna the reason for his and Claudette's presence in Croissant City, and Orchid's motive in permitting them to remain at 591 Funeral Street.

Belladonna shook her head and snorted.

"Mama will do anything to get her hands on that wretched fossil; it's downright weird. I can't tell you how many hours Beau and I have wasted searching through all this junk." She indicated their surroundings. "Through the whole house, in fact, before, of course, you went and found it, and . . ."

August grimaced, acknowledging his part in the recent loss of the precious gemstone.

"What is this place?" inquired August, removing his helmet and eyeing a cast-iron range buried beneath a stack of yellowed newspapers.

"The chauffeur would have lived up here," explained Belladonna briskly, "in the olden days. And before cars came along, it would have been the coachman. I expect this"—she patted the bench on which she was seated—"came from an old carriage.

"Now." The girl stood and wiped her hands on a rag. "I guess you'll want to sleep somewhere."

She crossed to a corner of the room where a door was partly visible behind the attic clutter. The girl used her body weight to shove aside a stack of boxes and cracked the door to reveal a small closet.

"If I remember correctly," she muttered, rummaging around with one arm. "Yes. Here it is." She awkwardly extracted a fold-up cot, well used, its enamel chipped. "There's only one, I'm afraid."

"That's all right," responded August. "Claudette prefers the floor. I think it reminds her of her tomb."

Belladonna grunted in reply as she heaved a box from the pile.

"We'll need to make some space for you. I can't imagine that anyone has slept up here in decades. You saw the state of that car downstairs."

"Let Claudette move those," suggested August. "She's mighty strong."

"I recall," said Belladonna archly, as she dumped the box near August's feet.

As she stooped, the top of the girl's head caught August's eye; a dark stripe ran along the parting of her hair.

Belladonna's roots were not blond, but brown.

"You dye your hair?" As soon as he'd said it, August felt self-conscious. It suddenly seemed like the sort of thing a person shouldn't really ask.

But Belladonna, as she straightened, seemed unruffled. She ran her hand through the honey waves and glanced up at them. She nodded with a small, bitter smile.

"I do. We do, Beau and me. She makes us. To look more like her. To look more like Malveaus."

August frowned, baffled. "But you are Malveaus."

Belladonna nodded slowly. "I suppose. Legally." She looked directly at August. "But . . . we're adopted."

August blinked, unsure how to proceed.

"Ah!" he said knowingly. He wanted to respond appropriately so proceeded with caution. "So, you're special." He smiled generously. "You were chosen. Specifically."

Belladonna did not return the smile.

"Chosen?" she wondered. "Or recruited? Recruited to be Malveaus; no, to be *perfect* Malveaus. To dye our hair Malveau blond. To act like Malveaus act and talk like Malveaus talk." She glowered at nothing in particular. "To be genteel and respectable, to wear black and endlessly mourn for a man we can't even remember." A muscle flexed in her jaw. "To be just . . . like . . . her."

"Well," August began quietly, "Beauregard is . . ."

"Just like her?" suggested Belladonna. "My brother loves to feel superior. He loves belonging to an old, highfalutin family." She glanced at August. "That's why he dislikes you so. You, cousin, are the real deal. Mama's blood runs through your veins. To be sure, it's DuPont blood—nuttier than a squirrel turd—but it's a darn sight fancier than mine and Beau's. Knowing that has Beauregard all twisted up like a salted pretzel with jealousy. He's insecure. That's why he's always so desperate for Mama's approval, why he's always trying to prove to her that he's a real Malveau."

Belladonna shook her head.

"But Beau doesn't get it. She doesn't see us as her children; not really. We're more like living dolls, to dress up in her image.

We're a living, breathing advertisement for Malveau perfection." She frowned. "Whether we like it or not."

A sudden clatter interrupted their conversation. Claudette had shifted enough boxes to create a space that permitted the closet door to swing fully open, and a suitcase had tumbled out, busting open and spewing its contents across the floorboards.

"Be more careful, Claudette!" admonished August, hurrying to scoop up the jumble of memorabilia: notebooks, withered corsages, and faded photographs.

Belladonna unfolded the cot.

"I think there's enough room here," she said. "And look!" She pointed through a small window revealed by Claudette's labors. "You can see the stars. It's like the St. Louis Hotel. There's even a little bathroom over there you can change in."

August emerged in baggy, oversized pajamas to find Claudette chomping on the hem of her borrowed nightgown and Belladonna tucking a sheet around the thin, moth-eaten mattress. For a moment, his cousin looked almost maternal.

A sudden, jarring *tring-tring* caused August and Claudette to jump.

Belladonna, with a surprised expression, looked around. She peered behind a steamer trunk, then a tower of hatboxes, and then, from inside a wicker baby stroller, she withdrew a pincushion, a rust-spotted flashlight, and, finally, an old-fashioned black dial telephone with a curly wire—the source of the high-pitched sound.

"Yes, Escargot?" she said into the receiver. "Oh, how peculiar. Well yes, I suppose, put her through."

Belladonna turned to August and held out the receiver.

"It's for you."

CHAPTER 17

NIGHTMARE

"I'll return your clean clothes in the morning," whispered Belladonna, "before breakfast."

August accepted the receiver gingerly and regarded it like the foreign object that, to him, it was.

"Hello?" he said cautiously, waving at his cousin's departing back. "Hello?"

Nothing.

"Who is this?"

Nothing again.

Then he detected a faint, shrill squeaking emanating from somewhere near his chin and realized he was holding the contraption upside down.

"August?" He heard a familiar voice brimming with shrill hysteria. "August? Is that truly you? Tell me, sugar, that you are quite safe, or I shall expire right here on the fainting couch at this very moment.

"How could you do this to me? Why would you do this to me? Oh, August, what will become of you? What will become of me?"

August waited patiently until the lady ran out of breath.

"Hello, Aunt Hydrangea," he responded calmly. "When did we get a phone?"

There was a moment's silence; the lady had clearly not anticipated this response.

"Why, sugar, we've always had a phone, someplace or other. Several, I imagine. It's a lack of phone line from which we at Locust Hole have suffered. A product, no doubt, of not paying our bill these past months. Or is it years? You know, it might just be a decade."

"How," August rephrased his question, "is it that you're able to make this call?"

"Why, that delightful Mr. LaPoste is here. And, August, he has given me use of his . . ." Her voice was muffled as she directed it elsewhere. "What do you call this device, Mr. LaPoste? A mobile phone you say?" Then louder. "His mobile phone, sugar."

"Why on earth," wondered August, "is the mailman there at such a late hour?"

"What's that, Mr. LaPoste? He says to tell you, August, that he received your note, that he will water your pepper plants, and that he is diligently keeping an eye on your aunt Hydrangea. Oh! Me? Why, that's most kind, Mr. LaPoste, but quite unnecessary."

August heard her giggle and felt a little nauseated.

"Now, August." Hydrangea refocused. "You get yourself back here to Locust Hole this very minute."

"I'm afraid that's impossible, ma'am." August patiently explained that he could not abandon his search, because he was unable to show up to his own life until he had rid himself of his tenacious undead ancestor, and to achieve this, he must locate and secure the Zombie Stone.

Hydrangea sighed, resigned. Another silence.

"And is she there, my sister?"

"Aunt Orchid has given us a place to stay."

"How does she look? And what of the house? Tell me every detail."

August began to relate his observations of the house on 591 Funeral Street, fielding Hydrangea's questions as best he could.

"Yes, the furnishings are very grand. Yes, there is still a harp in the music room. No, I will not kick Aunt Orchid under the table when no one's looking."

As he listened and obediently responded, August watched Claudette awkwardly recline on Belladonna's old carriage bench. She stuck the thumb of her dismembered arm into her mouth and sucked. August knew that this passive state was the closest the zombie came to sleeping. He wondered what she was thinking. Or *if* she was thinking.

Her drowsy air was infectious. August yawned and slumped onto the cot that Belladonna had unfolded and made up for him.

"It is getting late, Aunt. I'm sure Mr. LaPoste would like his phone back so he can get home."

A handful of memorabilia was still strewn across the floor, from the suitcase, August realized, that had tumbled from the closet. The boy pushed the postcards and photographs around with his toe.

"Yes, I promise to come home as soon as possible. I'll be sure to wear my helmet and gloves. No, I won't tell Aunt Orchid that."

Something suddenly caught August's eye.

"You too," he said absently. "Goodnight."

Eyelids drooping, August picked up an old, browned newspaper clipping.

He read the headline, yawning again, " 'After dramatic upset, local debutante wins Pepperville pageant.' "

The accompanying photograph featured a young woman wearing a sash embroidered with the words "Miss Chili Pepper

Princess." She was being crowned—presumably by the previous title holder—with a tiara that August immediately recognized as Hydrangea's. But the face below it belonged to someone else. The boy peered more closely.

"Why, Claudette," he said. "I think this is Aunt Orchid."

* * *

That night, August had strange dreams. Their soundtrack was the rustle of palm fronds from the courtyard, which occasionally morphed into the celestial strains of melancholy harp song.

He saw a crystal ball, a swirling mist within. Something began to materialize, a second orb, but of a lustrous amber, with a black spiral at its core, resembling an alligator's eye. The crystal ball evaporated, leaving only the Zombie Stone suspended in a velvety black vacuum.

August strove to reach it, struggling against a combative wind. The stone grew no closer. The palm fronds thrashed, and August could make no headway against the gale, which had grown frigid. His hands and feet felt frozen. He reached, straining, for the stone; through squinted eyes, he could see his own outstretched fingers. "My toes," he thought, "are so very cold."

The boy awoke with a start. He was sitting bolt upright in his cot, heart pounding. Beyond the small window, tossing palm fronds were silhouetted against the starry sky. His blanket had

w over

an Flu

ACK

ane Co.

After dramatic upset,
local debutante wins
Pepperville pageant

"It's just so very

ridden upward, exposing the boy's feet, and an icy draft had chilled his toes to a pale blue.

The distinct breeze appeared to originate from the closet immediately before him, for the door was open, and staring into it was Claudette.

CHAPTER 18

A SECRET PASSAGE

"Claudette?" The zombie turned to August with a low groan, while simultaneously pointing into the closet (inasmuch as zombies, with their claw-like, twisted fingers, *can* point). "You hear something?"

August slipped on his shoes and joined her at the end of the cot. The draft was strong enough that it rippled Claudette's nightgown.

Behind the boxes, cases, and tarnished golf clubs, August could see a brick wall. He glanced to his right, through the window, to observe the same brick extending along the east side of the courtyard.

"It's the back wall of the theater," he informed Claudette.

August lifted his nose into the current of cool air; it smelled of damp and papery decay.

"Remember," said August, "what Cyril Saint-Cyr said, about a secret passage?"

Together, the DuPonts hurriedly began to empty the closet of its contents.

"Belladonna," observed August, "said no one has slept up here in decades. If you weren't lying right in front of this closet, I reckon you'd never notice the draft."

The boy now stood immediately before the closet's cleared rear wall. He ran his palms across the worn brick.

"I can feel the air coming through here. And here. And down here."

August knocked, generating a weak, flat slap. Again. His third attempt produced a deep, resounding thud. He glanced at Claudette.

"Some of these bricks are just a veneer," he explained. "I think they might be cemented to a door." He continued knocking and pressing close to the sources of the draft.

Pop! A brick—or rather some moving part disguised as a brick—suddenly depressed beneath his touch and a good portion of the wall creaked open, swinging away into a dark void.

"Oh my," breathed August. "You didn't know about this, Claudette? Oh, right, how could you? You were dead long before your brother created it."

Feeling about the far side of the wall, August's palm located a cold, metal light switch. *Click!* Nothing. *Click! Click!* The void remained an inky, unwelcoming black.

"Now, where," wondered August, "is that rusty flashlight?" He exited the closet and made for the wicker baby stroller. "Belladonna will be so excited. We'll explore tomorrow when it gets light; maybe we can even get into the theater. Ah, here it is. Well, what do you know, Claudette; it still has some battery power.

"Claudette?"

August stared into the closet, which moments earlier had contained a small zombie and was now entirely empty.

"Oh, no." The boy sighed as he approached the dark opening. "You've got to be kidding me."

He held up the flashlight, sweeping its watery beam through the darkness. Several yards away it picked up movement: a shambling, ragged figure.

"Claudette!" hissed August furiously. "Get back here!" But the zombie grew smaller and dimmer. "Ugh!"

August let his head fall back in frustration . . . and entered the secret passage.

The floorboards creaked beneath his feet. August could hear the uneven, dragging progress of his undead relative somewhere up ahead.

"Claudette! Come back!"

The skimpy, flickering circle of light before him picked up a mouse scuttling along the baseboard and, on either side, mildewed wallpaper printed with an oppressive, organic pattern that appeared to warp and shift, forming ghoulish faces.

Here and there, the wall covering had been lacerated by ragged horizontal scratches like those made by animal claws.

"That," muttered August, pausing to study and touch one of the violent gashes, "does not look good."

A ghostly figure came into view, hovering aimlessly in the middle of the corridor.

"Claudette! You are in so much trouble. Seriously, you can't just wander off into dark passages like that. What are you looking at?"

August stooped to examine a crack in the floor. It was perhaps a quarter inch wide and dissected the floorboards in a perfectly straight line from wall to wall. From it rushed the pervading cool, damp, moldy air.

"The source, I guess," said August, "of the draft."

Claudette emitted a grunt of curiosity and August glanced up.

"What is that?" he said, pointing. "Right there, beside you?"

A round steel casing, drum-shaped, like the end of a soda can, was mounted on the passage wall at rib height. From its side protruded a short pipe with a plastic knob on the end. A double-ended arrow on the casing's face indicated that the lever moved from left to right.

Over this lever hovered Claudette's hand.

"Don't you do it, Claudette!" warned August. "I'm telling you, one time when Stella Starz pulled an unidentified lever, she released fifty racing pigeons . . . the day before the race!"

August stood, slowly, arms extended.

Claudette's fist closed over the plastic knob.

"I mean it, Claudette! Don't you pull that—aaaaargh!"

The floor beneath him instantaneously disappeared and August hurtled downward.

A moment later, when he gathered his senses, the boy found himself lying spread-eagle on a pile of mattresses. He was winded but unhurt. Far above him, Claudette's eyes were madly swiveling.

"Wha . . ." August forced himself into a seated position to discover that a double trapdoor had released him into a sort of cage suspended below the passage.

To his right lay a cold, impenetrable wall. He was otherwise surrounded by rigid vertical bars, and beyond those lay a lofty room, illuminated by a luminous shaft of moonlight piercing a skylight of wired glass. The corridor above him had clearly been borrowed from and framed within this much larger space.

August promptly shrieked. Hovering in the air several yards away was a phantom. The spirit was pale and insubstantial, with burning ice-blue eyes and a yawning black void where its mouth should be.

A moment later, the boy gasped in relief as his brain registered that the thing was two-dimensional. It was painted, part of a larger image depicting some creepy, nocturnal cemetery where other such spirits drifted skyward from their graves.

"This must be," August spoke upward, toward Claudette, "where they kept the theater scenery." Beyond the graveyard he could see the exposed edges of other enormous stacked backdrops: a fairy-tale forest, a Greek temple, what looked like part of a sun-bleached desert.

The musty odor was stronger here, the product, August guessed, of yards and yards of rotting painted canvas.

The boy stumbled awkwardly to his feet and staggered across the stack of mattresses, attempting to find his balance. Holding the bars, he looked down.

Some ten feet below him, on a cement floor, the remains of his flashlight were scattered. He looked up.

Some ten feet above him hovered Claudette's face, which appeared to register something close to alarm.

"You *should* look guilty!" August scolded the zombie crossly. "I told you about the racing pigeons." He sighed and looked around. "Okay, let's try this."

August grabbed a mattress and, rolling it into a loose cylinder, stuffed it into a corner to hold it in place. He repeated the process with a second and a third, and, stacking them on one another, attempted to scramble over and up, toward the square hole above him.

But the mattresses were uncooperative (as mattresses tend to be), sliding out from the pile and springing stiffly open, smacking the boy in the face.

He scowled up at Claudette, who, with a remorseful expression, lay facedown and reached into the cage.

"Ew! You're drooling, Claudette! This won't work; it's too far."

Nonetheless, the boy stood on tiptoe, one fist gripping an iron bar for support, straining toward the zombie's outstretched hand. August leaped as best he could from the limp, uneven mattress mess beneath his feet.

But his fingers and Claudette's were still feet apart.

The boy fell heavily back to the mattresses.

"I don't think," he said, looking up at the zombie with despair, "there's a way out!"

CHAPTER 19

A MELTED FACE

August leaned back limply, legs spread out.

"Is there anything," he wondered after a moment, "you could throw down that I could grab on to?"

With her attached hand, Claudette lifted her torso from the floor and twisted her head from side to side. She slumped back onto her chest, clearly employing her only active arm to reach for something nearby.

Suddenly the zombie's hand appeared again, fingers open, reaching down past the boards of the open trapdoor.

"No, no," said August. "We've tried that. You're too high up. I mean, is there like some rope or . . ." He stopped short as Claudette's hand descended farther and farther . . . and yet farther into the cage.

"Oh, I see." August grinned.

The descending digits belonged to the zombie's amputated arm, which she was extending into the space like a lifeline.

August groaned as, on tiptoe, he stretched upward, as far as he possibly could.

"Got it!" The boy's hand gripped the zombie's dismembered wrist. The zombie's dismembered hand gripped the boy's wrist. August's stomach lurched as he was yanked swiftly upward toward the ceiling, arced through the air, and landed facedown on the floor of the secret passage.

"Impressive," acknowledged the boy, brushing himself off at the edge of the impassable opening. "But in the future, let's leave strange levers alone." Reaching out, August gripped the handle on the wall and forced it toward its opposite extreme.

A strained creaking and electrical whir accompanied a sudden lurch from the trapdoors, which subsequently began to rise jerkily, propelled by obscured mechanics. But as the opening closed, an unanticipated consequence became immediately obvious.

"Uh-oh!" said August as the moonlight was promptly extinguished.

August thought of the broken flashlight somewhere twenty feet beneath them. His heart thumped hard, as anyone's might if they found themselves in an unfamiliar secret passage and unexpectedly plunged into total darkness.

"Claudette?" August reached for the zombie, and the feeling of her cold, lifeless forearm was vaguely comforting.

"I think," said August's bodyless voice, "it was this way back. Wait, where are you going? No, this way. Or was it this way? Oh dear."

Without any visual reference, August felt completely disoriented.

As his eyes grew accustomed to this new, lightless situation, they detected a thin red stripe several yards away.

"Can you see that, Claudette? What is that?"

Feeling his way along the jagged gashes in the wall, August headed for the crimson line and, within several shuffled yards, discovered that the corridor ended.

A sliver of dull red light escaped through a crack by the floor, suggesting that they had arrived at a door. And sure enough, beneath his palms, August detected peeling wooden panels and a metal knob.

"It's probably locked," speculated August. It wasn't. But before he pushed it open, August pressed his ear against the door to listen.

All footsteps and movements now stilled, silence closed in. August could hear his own heartbeat. He could hear an electric buzz, like that of a distant lightbulb. He could hear the minuscule displacement of air by the paper-thin wings of a solitary butterfly.

The brass within his fist was cold and hard. The floorboards seemed to press themselves against his feet. Or was gravity pressing him into them? He sensed some dull, distant throb, perhaps the very heartbeat of the earth.

Someone whispered in August's left ear, but Claudette, he knew, was on his right.

The boy was immediately reminded of his experience in the DuPont-Malveau family cemetery. He was reminded of Professor Leech's séance.

Something, August knew, was up.

He opened the door.

* * *

August felt for the light switch. It was unresponsive.

However, the reddish light escaping from around a second door opposite was enough to dimly illuminate the room before him.

August and Claudette descended a handful of steps into a modestly sized chamber, tightly crammed with an eclectic jumble of objects.

"This," observed August, "must be the old prop room."

Chairs, sideboards, and coat stands were stacked in towers, and the ceiling was concealed behind a canopy of unwired light fixtures in every possible style, from medieval to modern. Tangled throughout the crowded space was a collection of bizarre things: a suit of armor, a stuffed marlin, a barber's pole, and several mannequin torsos.

Whisper, whisper.

"Do you hear that?" August glanced at Claudette and was extremely surprised when she nodded. "You do? I'm not crazy?" The zombie shook her head.

"Hello? Is anyone in here?" August proceeded with caution toward the other door. He edged past a large mounted globe, upon which was perched a witch's hat.

"Argh!" The boy was startled when a figure lunged toward him, crashing to lie lifeless on the floor. The life-sized ballerina had a face that appeared to have melted, like a candle.

"Wax!" August informed Claudette, running his finger across what remained of the dancer's forehead.

"This one is locked," August announced, arriving at the second door.

He peered through the large keyhole. Immediately beyond lay a shadowy space of panels, raw timbers, and pulleys dangling from dark places. A few hangers still hung from a rolling coat rack, and a broken microphone lay on the floor.

Beyond this lay the larger expanse of a stage, its central portion concealed by barriers that appeared to form some sort of freestanding enclosure. Beyond the footlights lay the much grander reaches of a soaring auditorium.

The only light was red and provided by emergency exit signs. But it was enough to see that the place had been repurposed.

The rows of theater seating that would once have held an audience had gone, replaced by a complex maze of vertical partitions. Arranged within these, August could make out a shadowy, static populace of costumed figures.

Many were obscured by the system of cubicles. But others were partially visible in the crimson gloom, sporting crested helmets, imperial crowns, bishop's miters, and jauntily angled stovepipe hats.

"Saint-Cyr's Wax Museum," August said, turning to Claudette. "The famous and infamous, large as life in wonderful wax!"

He stood, turned, and surveyed the prop room.

"Well, that," he said, "certainly explains our ballerina friend."

Whisper, whisper.

"Who *is* that?" August was irritated now. Why was he hearing these pesky voices?

He navigated the muddle of props, peering into the darkest corners of the crowded room.

"Is someone hiding in here? Do you need help?"

Whisper, whisper.

The boy sidled into the narrow passages between the shelving systems loaded with bizarre bric-a-brac. At eye level August passed powdered wigs on stands, jars of false teeth and glass eyes (he pushed the latter out of sight, so that Claudette wouldn't be tempted to swap them out with her own), hands of wax, feet of wax, faces of wax, a grotesque grinning baby, a scowling old-timey police officer, a hollow-eyed young boy.

Whisper, whisper.

It was louder now. More insistent. Demanding even. August could almost identify some element of language.

His attention was captured by the sad-faced young boy before him. This wax sculpture seemed different from the others; more complex. More lifelike. August peered at it closely.

"Is that"—he extended an inquisitive finger—"even wax?"

But before he could find out, the boy's eyes snapped open.

CHAPTER 20

RUN!!!

August yelled and backed into the shelves behind him, knocking a toaster and a sharply jangling tambourine to the floor.

Over his shoulder popped a woman's face, or at least half a face, all flesh below the lady's nose having decomposed to expose her lower skull and jawbone. For a moment, August assumed that, like the ballerina, this was a damaged and unfortunate waxwork. But the moment was brief, for it immediately became clear that this woman was not formed from wax, being very much animated, her teeth clattering excitedly together, her eyes bulging and blinking.

Wigs, jars, and waxy body parts, skateboards, vases, and

electrical appliances began to shift and tumble and clatter. The two animated faces were clearly attached to animated bodies that were now extricating themselves from the objects around them.

August stumbled back through the shelves toward Claudette, narrowly dodging a bar stool dislodged by the abrupt emergence of a third awakening figure.

Claudette moaned pitifully, pointing toward a fourth.

As lamps and plastic fire hydrants and tennis rackets fell to the floor or crashed against walls, it felt as if the entire room had been magicked to life. Grunts, growls, and indescribable animal sounds accompanied the appearance of jerking angular limbs and fiercely flashing eyes.

A huge, powerful man loomed out of the shadows, his enormous, yellowed, withered hands extending toward August. The figure's swinging jaw and open mouth revealed scant but gruesome teeth, and he emitted a spine-chilling, soulless howl.

Other twisted, twitching persons appeared behind him.

"RUN!!!" screamed August, shoving Claudette toward the secret passage.

But the boy was half-blind and clumsy with panic and tripped, his limbs splaying across the handful of steps below the doorway.

He felt a cold and bony grip around his ankle and was promptly yanked backward. August screamed, grabbing at

the stair rails. But his assailant was powerful. A second mighty wrench was accompanied by a violent, splintering snap, and the boy was dragged backward again, this time with a broken bannister in his fist.

"Claudette!" he yelled.

Suddenly August's collar jerked against his throat as his pajamas were grabbed from above and his ankle was wrenched free. The next thing he knew, the boy was in the secret passage beside Claudette, who was slamming the door closed.

The DuPonts threw their shoulders against it as a mighty force struck the door from the opposite side, rattling August's teeth. Another blow knocked August to the ground. The third ripped the dry, termite-riddled wood away from the hinges.

August and Claudette fled back through the corridor, with only the dim red light from behind to guide them.

They were pursued by a cacophony of grunting and stumbling and the alarming sound of long, strong fingernails ripping along wallpaper.

"The trapdoor!" yelled August.

As he hurled himself against the wall beside the lever, it dawned on the boy that this was surely the very circumstance for which the devious device had been designed.

The ragged, shambling, drooling, wild-eyed, snaggletoothed horde of zombies (for surely it is now clear to all that this is what they were) was almost upon them.

August waited until he felt the first spatter of spittle on his face, then, with a primal yell, pulled the lever with all his might.

* * *

"I thought there were more of them," August observed to Claudette. "It seemed like there were more."

Four zombies, strewn awkwardly across the mattresses, ogled up at August from the suspended cage. Although similarly twisted and dilapidated, each was distinct in their state of decay and personal trappings.

One was a glum-looking young woman whose tasseled gown and feather headdress suggested the costume of a theatrical entertainer. The smallest of the zombies was the hollow-eyed boy, who was robed in the rich silks and ornate jewels of a foreign prince. The lady with but half a face sported a dapper hat and buttoned boots, which, despite her state of decomposition, lent her an air of fashionable respectability. The last and largest zombie, judging by his polka-dotted head scarf, swashbuckling coat, and knotted sash, was surely a pirate.

"Is that . . . no, it can't be," said August, frowning. "Is that the pirate Jacques LeSalt?"

At the mention of the name, the zombie's head cocked to the side.

"It sure looks like him; at least, how he'd look after being dead for a very long time." August scratched his head. "And the other ones, they look familiar too. The sad showgirl. The small prince. The half-faced lady."

August grabbed Claudette's arm.

"Madame Marvell's houseboat! The poster! DuPont's Dance of the Dead!" Claudette regarded August expectantly. "These," the boy explained, palms held forth toward the undead group, "are Orfeo's zombies! The deceased that he reanimated with the Zombie Stone, for diversion and delight."

He studied the zombies for a moment, and was struck, as he had been on his first meeting with Claudette, by their pathetic air. Tangled and tattered beneath him, the derelict creatures suddenly seemed far less fearsome than they had in the crowded and gloomy prop room.

"They must have been hanging around that storage room for"—August performed a mental calculation—"almost a hundred years! I guess people imagined they were props . . . or old waxworks. But why are they coming back to life now?"

August and Claudette observed with curiosity as the pirate scrambled about unsteadily on all fours, then gripped the cage bars in huge fists. Awkwardly, like a weird and jerking spider, the half-faced lady clambered onto his back.

"What are they doing?" wondered August. "Oh, wait. Oh, no!"

The showgirl was scrabbling onto the others, and the small prince onto her, forming a human tower. Five grubby little fingers appeared over the opening.

August slammed back the lever, but it was too late; as it grinded and whirred, the rising trapdoor was simply lifting the pile of zombies along with it.

* * *

"Use all your strength, Claudette!" cried August. "Every ounce."

The DuPonts were once again in the Malveaus' carriage-house closet. Claudette braced herself against the closed brick-clad door as August fumbled desperately around the edges searching for the concealed latch.

"Where is it? Oh, where is it?" he babbled in a panic. *Click.*

As he threw himself beside Claudette, August heard a dull thud and felt the faintest vibration. He glanced at his undead relative. Another thud, the faintest tremor.

"This one's much thicker than the prop room door," he said, nodding hopefully. "I'm sure it will hold."

With a violent crash, splinters of wood and brick went flying, and a yellowed, withered hand smashed through the door, grabbing August's arm in an enormous fist.

PART III

CHAPTER 21

FIVE ZOMBIES TOO MANY

"**B**ut you've only been here for one night!" Belladonna said in disbelief as she placed laundered clothing on the table. "How could you possibly have picked up four more zombies? Is that . . . Jacques LeSalt? Where the devil did you get them all?"

August was seated on the carriage bench, surrounded by a swaying, grunting, dribbling assortment of undead persons, who peered at and occasionally prodded him with something that seemed like curiosity.

The boy looked up at his cousin with resigned exhaustion.

"I found them in there." He indicated the open closet door. "Or maybe they found me. I'm not sure."

Belladonna walked over to gaze at the jagged-edged void that had been the rear closet wall.

"So," she muttered, mostly to herself, "there really was a secret passage. And the zombies were . . ."

"In the theater," confirmed August. "I guess these are the performers from Orfeo DuPont's Dance of the Dead. They must have been moldering back there ever since Orfeo left town. Whatever 'left town' means. That's how Mr. Saint-Cyr put it."

"Disappeared," muttered Belladonna absently, "would be more accurate." She turned back to August. "At least, that's what Mama told me. By all accounts, Orfeo DuPont set out on a fishing trip one day, with nothing but a packed lunch and a rod. No one ever saw him again."

"Well," grumbled August, "whatever became of him, he certainly left me with a mess bigger than a tick on a heifer's behind. Ow! Stop that!"

He smacked away the small prince's probing finger from his ear.

"You've got quite a fan club there," observed Belladonna.

"They've been at it all night. I tried to sneak out, but they follow me around like puppy dogs. Like they're obsessed with me. This is a disaster, I tell you! I can't even get rid of one!" August glanced resentfully at Claudette, who, perched on the cot, had discovered the Carnival bubbles in her pocket, and was repeatedly attempting (and failing) to jam the ring-shaped wand into the bottle's neck.

"Now I've got five. Five! That's five zombies too many, wouldn't you say? Why me? What do they want with me? As if the butterflies weren't troublesome enough. What will Aunt Orchid think? And Aunt Hydrangea." August's expression grew bleak. "Beauregard. Everyone!"

He looked at Belladonna imploringly.

"I have to find the gallery that bought your jewelry and my model. You really can't remember the name of the place?"

Belladonna shook her head apologetically.

"Gallery Macaroni? Macramé? Something like that." She shrugged her shoulders, uncertain. "We've searched the city," she assured him, "but there's no such place."

August sighed and bit his lower lip as he lifted Jacques LeSalt's withered hand out of his pajama pocket.

"That man who held the séance last night," the boy mused. "The . . . clairvoyant, is it? Mr. Slug or Snail or something."

"Professor Leech? Mama thought he might help her find the stone you're both so obsessed with."

"Yes, him. Do you know where I might find this professor?"

Belladonna shook her head.

"But Mama might."

August grimaced. He did not relish the prospect of seeking out his formidable aunt.

"Could you"—he winced—"watch my zombies while I go ask her? Make sure no one sees them?"

Belladonna regarded her cousin as she might a raving lunatic.

"I am quite sure I don't know how to entertain one zombie," she protested, "never mind five. Besides, as you say, they seem mighty fond of you. I doubt your undead friends will do what *I* tell them."

At that moment, from Claudette's direction, a flurry of bubbles danced through the air. The small zombie emitted a gleeful and self-satisfied gurgle.

The bobbing soapy orbs instantly attracted the other zombies' attention, as they had attracted Claudette's on first encounter. The undead creatures drifted, transfixed, toward the airy, flexible spheres, poking, grabbing, grunting, and starting with seemingly endless surprise when the bubbles popped.

"Well that," said August, cheering a little, "at least solves that."

"It does?"

August picked up his pile of laundered clothing.

"Claudette, give those bubbles to Belladonna. I'm sure she blows the best bubbles. All of you are going to love them!"

CHAPTER 22

THE STRINGS OF A
BROKEN HEART

Morning light filtered through the courtyard's palm fronds, replacing the winter chill with a welcome, sunny warmth. Beyond the crunch of gravel beneath his feet, August could hear another sound, repeated yet irregular—a slicing, whooshing, and light metallic clashing.

To enter the back door of 591 Funeral Street, one was forced to pass by the rear wing of the house, which extended down one side of the courtyard. Here, several dining chairs were clustered on the brick path before two sets of open French doors. Through these, August could see that a large dining table had been pushed aside to accommodate the activity from which the slicing, whooshing, clashing sound derived.

Two pirates were engaged in a sword fight, one advancing in aggressive attack, the other retreating in frantic defense. A third pirate stood facing the wall, admiring his distinctly crooked mustache in a gilt-framed mirror from which a sheer black cloth had been pulled aside.

"Hit!" announced the assailing pirate as the side of his slim blade whacked the ribs of his opponent.

"Ow! That hurt," protested his victim.

"What do you think?" the third pirate absently asked of the mirror. "Earring or no earring?"

Upon hearing their voices, August realized that the colorful buccaneers were in fact his cousin Beauregard and his friends, Langley and Gaston, all attired in costume. Beauregard was taking a victory lap, both fists in the air.

"Bloody Beau," he crowed, "claims another victim. He's the deadliest blade on the high seas! Come, come, Gaston." He leaped to the center of the room, feet spread, knees bent, his blade standing at attention before his face. "Let's go again."

"Ummm . . ." Gaston was hesitant.

"Fencing requires discipline," insisted Beauregard, "and precision. Now, en garde!"

"Shouldn't—shouldn't we," stammered Gaston, "be wearing those mask thingies?"

"The practice tips are on," responded Beauregard, touching

his finger to the rubber guard at the tip of his weapon. "Don't be a baby."

"Well, I don't really . . ."

"*Allez!*" bellowed Beauregard, dropping his saber to horizontal and lunging forward. He advanced, attacking savagely, sword thrashing this way and that. Gaston awkwardly scrambled backward, knitted cap bobbing frantically as he parried the incoming blows as best he could.

"Ow! No, wait. Ow! Ow! Stop!"

Porcelain, glass, and silver rattled alarmingly as Gaston backed into a slender-legged buffet. With a deft maneuver, Beauregard whipped the sword out of his opponent's grip. It cartwheeled through the air and came clanking to the floor. The side of Beau's saber was suddenly pressed against Gaston's ample cheek.

"Surrender?"

Gaston frowned stubbornly.

"Surrender, friend," Beauregard's voice was ominous. "Bloody Beau shows no mercy, and there's no one to help you now." He glanced behind him. "Is there, Langley?"

"Huh?" responded Langley, still considering the earring.

There was a metallic, slithering clatter as Gaston's blade suddenly returned across the floorboards to rest at Beauregard's feet. Baffled, the blond boy dropped his guard and turned to

discover the cause of this unexpected development. Gaston promptly snatched up the sword and poked the tip into Beauregard's chest.

"Hit!" he cried happily.

But his victory was dismissed with an absent swat of the hand. Beauregard was glaring at August in the doorway.

"Oh," said Beauregard with disdain. "It's you."

August was studying his cousin's head, wondering if the hat and pirate wig concealed dark roots.

Beauregard sneered darkly. "What are you looking at? Not enough butterflies for you?"

"N-n-no," stammered August. "I mean, nothing."

He turned to slip quietly away but, as he did so, caught Gaston's eye. The ginger-haired boy nodded, touching his sword to his forehead with a discreet smile of gratitude that caught August by surprise. He recalled Gaston's reluctance to participate in Beauregard's heartless game of catch with Claudette's eyeball.

August decided to remain where he was.

"Why," he asked cautiously, "are you all dressed this way?"

Beauregard crossed to the dining table, where he laid down his saber and picked up a bottle and a rag.

"These are our costumes for the Carnival Grand Parade," he said without looking at his cousin.

"The Weepy Widows," chimed in Langley, "always sponsor the best and biggest float."

August smelled the pungent odor of mechanical oil as Beauregard wiped down his blade.

"My grandmother," Langley explained with an air of boredom, "is the most generous contributor. She said they wouldn't see a penny from her unless they gave us all a spot on this year's float."

"I don't see why," grumbled Beauregard, snapping the cap back on the oil bottle, "they had to have some stupid cat as grand marshal."

"Officer Claw?" said August in surprise. "He's amazing. A shining example to feline-kind across the universe. I can't wait to meet him."

"Meet him?" Beauregard spun around, sword in hand. "Why would *you* meet him?"

August hesitated, sensing danger.

"Um . . . well . . . Claudette won us places on the same float."

A beet-red flush coursed up Beauregard's neck and into his cheeks.

"You?" he said incredulously. "And that *thing*—that putrid undead DuPont monster? On *our* float? Well." Beauregard, shaken, searched for thoughts and words. "You won't come.

You can't come." He waved his saber vaguely at August, who had concealed the bulk of himself behind the doorframe.

"But," August muttered meekly, "we won the tickets fair and square. Officer Claw is my hero. Well, one of them. Certainly, my cat hero. I wouldn't miss it for the world."

Simmering, Beauregard slowly crossed the room. Only the right side of August's face was now visible.

"If that raggedy, stinking zombie"—Beauregard placed his sword tip on the doorframe, inches from August's nose—"embarrasses us in any way . . ." He leaned into the sword with such force that it bowed alarmingly.

"I'll find the Zombie Stone," August promised hoarsely. "It will solve everything."

"If you shame this family . . . again. If you ruin this for me . . ." Beauregard's expression was as dark as thunderclouds. "Then, I'll, I'll . . ."

Beauregard's sword snapped in two.

* * *

August hesitated, his fist on the knob of the back door. But his dread of confronting Orchid was outweighed by the urgency of finding the Zombie Stone.

As he entered the house, the boy was instantly transported to his nightmare of the previous evening, for he heard the strains of a harp—light and celestial, yet deeply resonant. He realized suddenly that the music in his dream had not been dreamt, for the melody he heard now was the same one: beautiful, but of a crushing sadness that was close to unbearable. Despite himself, August's eyes were suddenly hot with tears.

The music room was thick with the scent of gardenias, and August was surprised to discover that the musician was a familiar figure in black gown and veil. Her posture and aura were so altered, however, that for a second August wondered if this was indeed his aunt Orchid. Her neck was bowed, so he could not see his aunt's face, but her shoulders and back seemed heavy, as if burdened by a thousand sorrows. Her slender fingers moved with a leaden elegance, as though coaxing the mournful tune from the strings of a broken heart.

Orchid looked up, suddenly aware of a presence, and for the briefest of moments, August saw fatigue and frailty and sadness in her face. But it was replaced almost instantly with the cool and inscrutable Malveau composure.

Immediately behind her hung the portrait of Orchid's family before it was visited by tragedy, and August was again struck by the contrast of the woman today and the softer, carefree one of yesteryear. She reminded him of the girl featured in the carriage house newspaper clipping, the girl smiling breathlessly as she was crowned with a tiara.

"What are you doing in here?" Orchid asked impassively, standing and rubbing her long fingers.

"Why," asked August, emboldened by genuine curiosity, "is there an old picture of you in Aunt Hydrangea's tiara and sash? It was Hydrangea who won the Miss Pepper Princess pageant." He paused. "Wasn't it?"

Orchid picked up her palmetto fan and slipped into a chair by the fireplace, fanning herself. She smiled strangely.

"Hmm," she said, eyeing August, clearly contemplating what to say next. "No, August," she said matter-of-factly, "it was not. I won the pageant."

August gaped, unconsciously stepping forward.

"What? But she wears that tiara all the . . . It's her whole . . . I mean, it's who she *is*!"

Orchid nodded.

"It is true that she was a contestant. And she was quite disagreeable to her own sister, to me, when I entered to compete against her."

"I can kind of see," August suggested cautiously, "why that might upset her. Why did you enter, ma'am?"

Orchid looked away quickly, studying her fan.

"It's a free country, is it not?" she said irritably. "Why should Hydrangea's happiness be of more consequence than mine?"

"So . . . why does she *think* that she won?"

Orchid sighed, fanning herself. "After I left Locust Hole, she became increasingly, well"—she glanced at August—"the way she is now. She was convinced that the pageant had been stolen from her. That the tiara was rightfully hers. That she had been . . . betrayed."

Orchid softly snorted.

"My life had moved on. I had a husband. The twins. Château Malveau. What did I care about some small-town competition and a rhinestone trinket? So"—she shrugged—"I let her have it: the tiara, the title, the illusion. All those around her indulged the fantasy, unwilling to deny her some small victory."

August ran his finger down a nearby column, feeling a sense of guilt. He was beginning to realize that his caregiver was even more fragile than he had understood.

"Poor Aunt Hydrangea," he muttered. "She depends on me; I should never have left her. Perhaps . . . perhaps I should go home."

"Hydrangea," observed Orchid, "is likely stronger than you imagine. Besides, I thought you were set on finding that little chunk of Cadaverite for your loving aunt Orchid?" She spoke with the quiet intensity of a coiled cobra. "To—what was it—make up for past mistakes?

"Who knows, child, what rewards might await the party that fetches me that particular jewel?"

The woman locked eyes with her nephew, and August was reminded of her intimidating power of persuasion. What was she implying, he wondered? School again? Money? It was within her power, he was certain, to make Hydrangea's life a less impoverished one.

He considered too his own mission: to rid himself of increasing numbers of highly inconvenient zombies.

"I am, ma'am," he agreed, nodding, "set on finding the Zombie Stone." He straightened, recalling his purpose in seeking out his aunt. "I thought I might start with Professor Leech; he didn't really get to finish his reading last night. Do you know how I might find him?"

Orchid scoffed.

"Leech? Champagne Fontaine is a nitwit for trusting that oily fraud. I doubt he'll be of much use to you."

August shrugged. "It's a start."

"Very well." Orchid flapped her fan toward the foyer. "The so-called gentleman likely left his calling card. Try the silver tray in the foyer."

CHAPTER 23

SAD CELESTE AND BATISTE BAGUETTE

"No, I can't watch them any longer, I'm sorry," said Bella-donna, checking her watch. "I have . . . an appointment. It's important; I can't miss it. Besides, we're all out of bubbles." She turned the plastic bottle upside down to illustrate. "You'll just have to take them with you to Professor Leech's place."

August eyed his shoddy band of zombies, and his shoulders slumped.

"It shouldn't be that difficult," said Belladonna, moving to the small window by the closet. "As you say, it's like they're ob-sessed with you; they'll follow you like puppy dogs."

"That," grumbled August, "is exactly the problem."

"The courtyard's empty." Belladonna was peering down-ward. "There's no one to see if you leave now. There's a box of free tourist maps attached to the lamppost on the corner of Funeral Street."

* * *

August was forced to concede that Belladonna had been correct. Wrangling the ungainly crew of zombies through the crowded streets of the Old Quarter was less difficult than he'd anticipated.

Despite the crush of Carnival revelers in the streets, his un-dead entourage had a remarkable capacity for remaining close to him. It was almost as if the boy acted like a zombie mag-net. Moreover, the sheer number of merrymakers in costume—many of a ghoulish bent—rendered the zombies inconspicuous. Well, almost.

The group's appearance was extreme, even for Carnival, and it did attract more than its fair share of enthusiastic reactions.

"Awesome costumes, dudes!"

"The undead RULE!"

"Party on, zombie friends!"

At one point, August and his zombies found themselves surrounded by a raucous but agreeable gaggle of flush-faced young people, cans installed on the sides of their drink-guzzler helmets, who whooped and chanted, "Jacques LeSalt, Jacques LeSalt, Jacques LeSalt!"

"Up here, Jacques!" they cried, multiple palms rising to high-five the bewildered but cooperative pirate zombie.

In the lee of a restaurant chalkboard sign, August stopped to get his bearings. He looked at Leech's calling card. He glanced at the street signs attached to a nearby lamppost, then studied his map.

"It should be," he muttered, "just around this corner. Come along. Wait! One, two"—he counted off the zombies with his finger—"three, four. Me. That's only five; we're one down. Where's the miserable one?"

He glanced around, searching for the balding showgirl, and, above the crowds, spotted a flamboyant but scraggly feather headed into the open doorway of a townhouse on the opposite side of the street.

"Dang it," said August. "Where's she headed? Come on! Hurry, you guys! This way."

But by the time August had herded the company through the milling pedestrians, the entrance was blocked by a group of well-fed tourists in Croissant City T-shirts. Several were devouring bright icy treats in paper cups, purchased—August assumed—from the store that occupied the building at street level named Jo-Jo's Snow-Bombs.

"Ah, latecomers!" announced a familiar voice from somewhere near the townhouse door. "Well, I never! If it isn't Claudette DuPont and her great-great-nephew, August."

The well-fed tourists turned to look and, as they did so, created a line of vision.

"Oh! Hello, Mr. Saint-Cyr," said August, nodding self-consciously to all the curious faces staring at the fluttery activity above his head. Claudette waved her amputated arm in greeting, and Cyril Saint-Cyr chortled with delight.

"Now that, folks," he informed the tourists, "is how we do costumes in Croissant City! Well done, young lady."

"Um," explained August, "we're looking . . ."

"For the home of Sad Celeste?" suggested Saint-Cyr loudly. "Well, friends, you have come to the right place. We are just commencing the tour."

The gentleman raised a wooden paddle, much like one might use for table tennis, but with an extended handle and bearing faded letters reading "tour guide."

"Folks, please finish up those tasty snow-bombs. It's unseasonably warm today, and we wouldn't want them melting all over the museum, would we? Now, if you can't see me, just look out for this paddle."

It was impossible, in terms of both physics and manners, for August and his entourage to push past the plug of tourists, so with little choice, they joined the tour.

Another metal plaque was screwed into this building's brick façade. It read "Old Quarter Historical Monument Number Thirty. The Sad Celeste House."

A narrow interior staircase opened into a generous apartment above Jo-Jo's Snow-Bombs. Sunlight passing through lace curtains scattered fragile shadows across the place, which, despite the ample furnishings, had an air of hush and abandonment. Velvet ropes suspended between short steel posts separated visitors from gleaming rosewood furnishings and delicate porcelain antiques.

"Above the mantel in the parlor," announced Saint-Cyr, "hangs a portrait of the apartment's prior resident: the lovely lady known as Sad Celeste."

August gasped. The attractive young woman depicted in a feathered headdress was clearly his missing zombie (prior, that is, to having become one).

"This," he hissed to Claudette, "was her house?"

"Miz Celeste," Saint-Cyr continued, "was a dancer with the French Follies and, in her day, the greatest star of the Theatre Français. She was celebrated far and wide for her beauty and grace. Observe"—Saint-Cyr swept his paddle around the space— "the floral carpet, the pianoforte, the finest bone china dinnerware, all gifts from Celeste's many rich and important admirers."

August, keeping a watchful eye on the tour guide, peered discreetly behind settees and Japanese screens. Claudette ogled him expectantly, but August shrugged.

"I don't see her anywhere," he whispered. "Where could she have gone?"

"But such exquisite, expensive tokens could not buy the lady's heart"—Saint-Cyr grew pensive and pressed the paddle to his chest—"for it was already given to another; to Batiste Baguette, a Frenchman of little fortune, and, sadly, a shiftless gambler."

As they ascended a second staircase, Saint-Cyr's commentary continued.

"Despite these obstacles, the pair seemed hopelessly in love and quite inseparable, until one day, the young man bid Celeste farewell, promising to soon return with a ring of betrothment."

He crossed the third-floor landing, stopped before a closed door, and turned with a somber expression to his audience.

"The lady never laid eyes on her beau again." He turned the knob.

Inside, the high-ceilinged room contained a dressing table littered with crystal jars and perfume bottles, a spindly bamboo washstand, and a slender four-poster bed, concealed on all sides by faded damask draperies.

"Decades later"—Saint-Cyr shook his head—"Batiste Baguette's name was discovered on the passenger list of a gambling ship named the *Lady Luck*. Sadly, the craft was anything but lucky. One fateful day, several miles from here, its boilers exploded, and the *Lady Luck* sank. There were no survivors. Historians have since suggested that Batiste was on board that fateful day to win back the promised ring, which he had recently lost in a bet. But, ignorant of this"—Saint-Cyr sighed deeply—

"Celeste believed herself forsaken; that her young man had tired of her and run off. Day after day, month after month, she pined out here"—Saint-Cyr crossed the room to indicate, beyond the French doors, a balcony suspended above the street—"weeping and lamenting so that the townsfolk came to name her Sad Celeste."

Cyril Saint-Cyr, museum guide, crossed to the bed.

"The story ends," he said with deep emotion, "one tragic morning, with a chambermaid discovering Celeste, cold as a pineapple Jell-O mold. She had wept herself to death, right here in this very bed."

With a theatrical gesture, Saint-Cyr swept back the damask draperies. Beyond them was not an unoccupied bed of crisply made-up linens, but rather, a blotchy, balding figure with skeleton hands who, startled by the sudden intrusion, snatched up the coverlet to conceal herself.

Saint-Cyr screamed.

The zombie screamed.

The tourists screamed.

The zombie screamed some more, a black cloud of flies escaping from her gaping, mottled mouth.

Saint-Cyr screamed some more.

The tourists screamed some more . . . and then they panicked.

One knocked over the washstand. One fell backward over

a velvet rope. Crystal jars and perfume bottles crashed to the floor. One compact but seemingly powerful woman shoved Cyril Saint-Cyr face-first into a wall in a desperate attempt to escape the room.

As the stampeding footsteps receded down the stairs, the only people that remained in the disheveled space were August and his zombies. The boy, who in the chaos had been knocked to the floor, rose and dusted himself off, glaring with frustration at his undead companions.

Zombie Sad Celeste sniffled, peering over the coverlet with red-rimmed eyes and a thoroughly dejected expression. August, shaking his head with resignation, plonked himself on the edge of the bed.

"It's . . ." He paused, searching for words. "It's okay, Celeste," he said, patting the thin bones of her skeletal hand. "I know this was your bedroom. But you don't live here anymore. Technically, you don't really live anywhere."

Celeste heaved a ragged sigh.

"I'm sorry about Batiste Baguette," August added gently.

Celeste lowered the coverlet.

"But at least," August said, smiling, "you have me now. Let's see about getting you to your real home, shall we?"

CHAPTER 24

THE CAMERA BOTANICA

August pointed at a street sign formed from decorative painted tiles cemented into a wall.

" 'Treasure Alley,' " he read aloud. "This is it. Now, do we have everyone?"

The company quit the sunlight and hubbub of the busy avenue for the shade and quietude of a narrow street. Above them, the iron balconies on opposite sides of the lane were so close, one might easily have jumped from one to another. The quarters were so tight that when proceeding, August and the zombies were forced to skirt a cluster of empty tables and chairs outside the Gold Doubloon Café and navigate a series of potted palms that lined the alley.

On one side, wedged between taller buildings, was a single low-slung and crumbly cottage with crooked, peeling shutters. It had the feeling of a thing outgrown by its surroundings. The single window displayed a dusty, sun-faded array of jarred candles, creepy-looking dolls and figurines, and a human skeleton painted with rainbow colors. August observed an oval sign hanging from the eaves above him that read "Leech's Camera Botanica."

" 'Camera,' " the boy explained to Claudette, just in case she was interested, "is an old word for a room. I saw it on *Are You a Dummy?* A botanica is a place that sells herbs and stuff."

A bell softly tinkled as August entered. The warm and claustrophobic interior could scarcely accommodate the living boy and his less-than-living companions. Jacques LeSalt's moaning head was lost in the froth of dried plants and herbs that obscured the low ceiling, and August found himself bumped by awkward undead limbs into shelves packed with labeled jars and bottles of colorful powders and liquids.

To steady himself, the boy grabbed hold of a stand displaying books with titles such as *Harnessing Magic in Talismans, Charms, and Amulets; Adder's Tongue to Witch Grass: A Handbook of Conjure Roots;* and *Necromancy for the Total Beginner.*

Suddenly, in the darkest corner of the store, the soft movement of a black curtain caught August's eye, and a figure wearing a light, rumpled linen suit appeared.

"Professor Leech," exclaimed August, "you might remember me from—"

"From Funeral Street," Leech interrupted. "Orchid Malveau's séance. How could I forget the face in the Oraculum's apparition?"

But Leech scarcely looked at August, gazing instead beyond him, transfixed by the tattered characters at his rear.

"I had no idea why"—he irritably swatted aside a butterfly, as if it were an unexpected and unwelcome intruder—"the ball might offer up your image." The light of a jar candle flickering near the cash register danced in the man's bulbous, watery eyes.

"But the Oraculum's power can be at times difficult to harness. Its visions are not always intended for the client. Sometimes they are meant for me." He slowly rubbed his hands together. "And I wonder, in this case, if the ball has brought you to me"— Leech shot August an oily smile—"for a reason. Tell me, young man, why is it that you have sought me out?"

"Well, sir," August ventured. "Do you know anything about zombies?"

"Why, naturally," said the professor. "I'm a professor!"

He was squeezing himself around the gaggle of moldy visitors, eyeing them up and down at close quarters with unconcealed fascination. The zombies huddled together, disconcerted by the intimate inspection.

"Zombies," explained Professor Leech, "are corpses that

have been reanimated by the spirit—or soul if you prefer—they once housed, that spirit having been drawn back into the mortal world by the magnetic pull of a Go-Between. And it would appear"—Leech came to a stop before Jacques LeSalt—"that you have brought me some fine specimens."

August nodded, hurriedly explaining his predicament and the resulting urgency of locating a particular Go-Between known as the Zombie Stone.

"It was sold inadvertently to a local art gallery. Oh, and by the way," August added, "it's what my aunt Orchid is after too."

Leech, fingering the buttons on the pirate's coat, nodded sympathetically.

"Orfeo DuPont's infamous Go-Between," he said absently, "with which he controlled—and indeed *created*—the undead."

"You know of it?" August was not entirely surprised, as everyone except August seemed already to be familiar with the famous fossil.

"This city, young man," Leech chuckled, "delights in its darkest corners. Every other house in the Old Quarter boasts an iron plaque, claiming it to be haunted, or the site of a long-ago murder or some other bloody, lurid incident. Our most celebrated residents are ghosts and witches and"—he paused, considering the fidgety pirate—"the undead. Even an *amateur* historian would recognize Jacques LeSalt here."

Leech gave Jacques a friendly poke.

"Tell us where your treasure's buried, eh, Jacques?" The pirate shrank into the other zombies, whimpering, his head lolling loosely about.

"So"—Leech abruptly diverted his full attention to August—"you have not located this art gallery?"

"Its name," explained August, "is something like Gallery Macaroni. Or Macramé."

Leech's brow arched with a flicker of something that looked like recognition. But it was quickly replaced by a frown.

"You've heard of it?" said August.

Leech shook his head.

"No. Sorry. I have not. But let us see what the Oraculum has to show us. How did these butterflies get in here?"

The ball-reading room was little more than a closet concealed behind the black velvet curtain at the rear of the botanica. The tight space accommodated only two chairs and a table, upon which sat the crystal ball of mesmerizing depth named the Oraculum. Leech sat, indicating that August should too. The zombies, unable to enter the tight space, clustered anxiously in the doorway, wrestling with the curtain and causing it to strain at the nails supporting it.

August glanced around at the black walls and a shelf crammed with seemingly unrelated objects: a crudely carved angel, an empty champagne bottle, a yellow jar candle bearing an image of the grim reaper.

Leech placed the sides of his hands on the scarlet tablecloth, palms facing the crystal ball. August traced his finger along the fabric's curious pattern of dragons and chrysanthemums.

"The Oraculum," began Leech, and again, his voice was quiet yet penetrating, "came before everything. The Oraculum sees worlds and times beyond this one. The Oraculum never lies."

Dropping his head, Leech glared intently into the ball. His eyebrows knitted. His fists clenched. A vein in his wrist throbbed.

Gazing into the bottomless void at the center of the glass sphere, August again experienced a sense of vertigo.

Whisper, whisper.

"Here we go again," thought the boy. And indeed, for a moment or two, the whispering gathered and intensified. But this time, the phenomenon was fleeting and abruptly passed. Whatever had been present was gone.

"Show us, great Oraculum," Leech commanded, "where lieth the stone of zombies."

Nothing happened.

"SHOW US!" the professor bellowed, causing August and the zombies to practically jump out of their skins.

Mists gathered, but they were thin and weak, less dense and animated than their showing at the séance. Leech's eyes widened, reflecting the dull glow of the Oraculum.

"I see . . . ," the professor said slowly. "I see a metal path.

A path across water. It's a bridge. No. A pier. A floating dock where vessels may anchor."

August peered more closely into the weak vapors.

"I don't see anything at all," he said.

"The secrets of the Oraculum"—Leech glared from under his eyebrows—"are not always revealed to the untrained eye."

"Oh!" August nodded intelligently, as if this made perfect sense.

"I see a sign," Leech continued, "in the form of a large sea-bird."

"Do you," August asked breathlessly, "recognize the place, sir?"

Leech looked grave.

"I do, young man. This is Pelican Wharf, and it is right here in Croissant City. The Oraculum never lies."

"So you've said," said August.

"What you are seeking," Professor Leech assured him, "lies there."

CHAPTER 25

ARMADILLO PEOPLE

"It's much farther than I thought," admitted August, consulting a scrap of notepaper with some handwritten directions. "Professor Leech didn't include any distances."

August and the zombies were making slow progress along a bleak and lonely road, flanked by rusting train tracks, vast warehouses, and silently towering cranes. Beyond a persistent weed or two, there was little in the way of greenery.

There were no other pedestrians, nor human activity of any kind other than a few occasional cars, some of which slowed down as they passed. August glimpsed one driver—a woman in a hat so flowery that it resembled an azalea bush—peering at the group in openmouthed amazement before abruptly speeding off.

The area seemed devoted to large industrial activities of a daytime nature and, in the gathering shadows of dusk, had taken on the deserted air of a ghost town.

"I didn't imagine," said August apologetically, "it would take this long to walk here. Not that we have enough money for a taxi anyway."

The nearby rails began to rattle and whine, the volume increasing rapidly.

"Here comes another one," warned August, covering his ears.

The zombies huddled behind him, clearly agitated by the clattering din of the passing freight train. Only Claudette appeared unworried, eagerly waving her detached arm at the graffiti-covered boxcars.

The last car, the caboose, trundled past, and beyond it was revealed a boxy, windowless building.

"Over there," commanded August.

He pointed to the faded lettering above the corrugated doors that read "Pirate's Sea Cargo" and bustled the zombies across the tracks into a sprawling parking lot.

The concrete expanse was empty but for one battered truck at the far side. The vehicle was growing hazy as it was engulfed by mist creeping from the nearby banks of the Continental River. As they passed it, heading into the wall of damp and chilly fog, August wondered why the tailgate of the unattended truck sat open, and what the boxes stacked nearby might contain.

He could now hear the lap of river waves, and the parking lot ended abruptly in an impassable thatch of reeds and shrubbery. The only route forward was a narrow metal walkway that disappeared into the swirling mist.

"This is it," August announced, peering up through the milky haze at a sign mounted on a post. The worn wooden plaque had been created in the shape of a pelican and bore signage indicating one's arrival at Pelican Wharf.

The rusty ramp groaned and creaked metallically as the party moved awkwardly along it.

"Shhh!" hissed August, turning to the zombies with a finger pressed to his lips. He was not sure why exactly, but the muffled silence of the fog made him self-conscious of the noise they were generating.

Through the painted metal grille beneath August's feet, dark ripples hinted at the presence of muddy water below. From the shallows on either side protruded strange, enormous nests of tangled, rotting timbers—the foundations, August guessed, of riverside structures long gone.

The gangway deposited August upon a metal platform, its surface patchy with rust and puddles. From the bobbing sensation beneath his feet, August could tell that they had arrived upon a floating pontoon.

The zombies, not the most stable at the best of times, were wobblier than ever and clung to the boy and to one another for support. As Jacques LeSalt grabbed August's shoulders from behind, the boy was thrust forward slightly and, in a puddle before him, saw something that jolted his senses.

A reflection stared back at him of a young girl near his elbow. The child had clear eyes, shiny brown ringlets, and a crisp, clean bow tied at the back of her head. The girl was healthy, flushed, and very much alive.

"Claudette?"

August turned sharply to his right, and there in the dimensional world stood his own pallid, drooling zombie, her loose eyes struggling to meet his own. She bent down, and as she did so, the other, pretty, puddle Claudette simultaneously bent up.

August was stunned. Somehow, in her reflected self, Claudette appeared as she had in life, before she was undead; before she was even regularly dead. Had he never, the boy wondered, seen her reflection before? He could not think of a moment when he had.

The physical Claudette was groaning softly. The puddle Claudette's mouth was moving.

"Are you saying something?" August asked in wonder, leaning in close. He heard a whisper, but this one was soft and musical, like that of a child, free from the wet gurgling of a zombie. "Louder," he urged. "It sounds like . . . 'pearls.' Are you saying pearls? You want your pearls back?"

But the conversation was abruptly interrupted when the

platform suddenly rose then fell on some watery surge and the half-faced lady stumbled, obliterating the puddle Claudette beneath her high-heeled boot.

Before the water could settle, before even August could give the strange incident further thought, the boy was presented with a more immediate situation.

"Who's there?" cried an unfamiliar and forceful voice from somewhere in the fog. "Show yourselves!"

The man's blurred silhouette emerged farther along the pontoon. August moved toward him, but his heart skipped a beat when, as the figure took form, he could see that its face and head were not those of a man.

Two pointed ears protruded from the creature's skull, a long snout extended toward August, and all were covered with an armor of thick scales. Worse, August could now make out similar figures lurking in the fog and, beyond them, the mass of a vessel tethered to the wharf, looming outriggers suggesting its function as a shrimping boat.

"Who is it?" inquired a harsh female voice emitting from a snouted figure on the vessel's stern who was accepting a box from another blurry figure on the wharf. "Is it the cops?"

"Nah," responded the closest creature. "Looks like some tourists from the Carnival. Cool costumes actually. Staggering drunk, I reckon. Some of 'em anyway."

Below the unsettling snout moved a very human mouth and a very human chin, and August's alarm dissipated as he realized that the man and his companions were wearing masks molded in the form of armadillo faces.

"You folks best be getting along now," said the armadillo man flatly. "It can be dangerous round these parts."

"We're looking," August explained politely, "for a large amber marble, sir. It's formed from a mineral called Cadaverite."

"Cadava-what?"

August peered past the man and into the fog, where other shadowy armadillo people continued to toil, passing box after box into the shrimping boat.

"The last time I saw it," he continued, "it was mounted on a model, like a balloon, with a skeleton boy."

The man scoffed.

"Skeleton boy?" He turned his head slightly to yell over his shoulder. "Virgil, you seen any skeleton boys round here?"

The stouter shadow, who was passing another box to the woman in the boat, guffawed loudly, and then, as a result, lost his grip.

"Dagnabbit!" snapped the man, presumably Virgil.

The box thumped onto the shrimping boat's washboard, where it burst open, a shimmering cascade of gold coins slithering forth.

Suddenly, with a spine-chilling, unearthly howl, the zombie pirate Jacques LeSalt lunged forth, knocking aside August, the armadillo man, Virgil, and the woman on the boat.

The grunting, loose-jawed pirate roughly righted the box and with his large-yet-withered hands began to scoop great piles of the coins into the air. He went in for more, letting the booty fall around him, and then again and again in a wild-eyed frenzy.

"Thief!" screamed the woman.

"Stop him!" yelled another voice.

In moments, many powerful armadillo-people hands had seized the undead pirate, yanked him from the vessel, and roughly tossed him onto the wharf, where he sprawled in an angular pile near August's feet.

"Hey!" protested August. "He's just a zombie, you know. He probably thinks that's his long-lost treasure. You don't need to be so—"

August stopped short. The first armadillo man had stepped forward threateningly. And, for the first time, August noticed a baseball bat in the man's fist. The man was close now—close enough that when it swung gently upward, his bat's tip was pressed against August's chest.

"Why you really here, huh?" The man's tone was low, dark, and threatening. "You come looking to steal from us? From the Armadillo Gang?"

"You show 'em, Homer," Virgil advised.

The baseball bat shoved August backward into the gaggle of fidgeting, trembling zombies at his rear.

Suddenly a blurred shadow darted in from the right.

There was a "HEY!" from Homer, followed by a powerful *whoosh* and a sickening crash.

Claudette stood holding the baseball bat's handle in the fist of her severed arm. The rest of the weapon lay in splinters, scattered across the undulating pontoon. But Homer did not flinch. He merely smiled coldly, growling softly, like a feral cat.

"So that's how you want this to go."

Slowly, from the inside of his long coat, the man drew a very large wrench. Behind him, armadillo people loomed from the fog. August counted at least five and, behind them, several more advancing smudges. All of their silhouettes had ominous extensions whose fuzzy forms suggested boat hooks, crowbars, and something that was possibly a toilet plunger.

"I told you these here was dangerous parts," said Homer. "They say this is Armadillo Gang territory. They say messing with the Armadillo Gang can get you hurt."

Homer smacked the wrench into his other palm with a vicious sneer.

"It's true, bro, I know it," said another voice—a high-pitched wheeze—from behind August. "It can get you hurt real bad."

August twisted swiftly around and was surprised and alarmed, based on the smallness of the voice, to discover the largeness of the advancing shadow.

The figure was taller even than Jacques LeSalt, and four times as wide, with shoulders and arms thick as those of a gorilla, arms that might toss any person present into the river like an old sweater.

"But no one," announced the newcomer, "is getting hurt tonight."

And, as he emerged into view, August beamed with delighted recognition and called out the ginormous man's name with unconcealed relief.

"Buford Juneau!"

CHAPTER 26

THE *SEA HAG*

August knew that they were headed back toward the Pelican Wharf ramp, but the fog had thickened and was now so dense, he could see only a few feet in front of him.

Buford, however, strode forth, his boots carelessly splashing through puddles with the confidence of a person who knew where they were going. So August hurried the zombies along in the wake of the Pepperville tattooist's immense, comforting shape.

"What brings you to Croissant City, Buford Juneau?" asked August breathlessly as he scurried to keep pace.

"Carnival, bro," responded Buford without looking down. "Those tourists sure do love them some temporary tattoos. Make a killing every year, I reckon, with my booth in LeSalt

Square. Lawyers, bookkeepers, geography teachers: they all pay me to ink 'em up with their favorite bands or cartoon characters. Makes 'em feel like somebody else." He chuckled. "Somebody dangerous. At least for a day or two. Till the tattoo wears off in the shower 'course."

He pointed to a spot underneath the metal ramp, where welcoming golden lights peeked through the fog.

"Looks like we're home."

As they passed beneath it, August heard a faint creaking on the steel walkway, and he glanced up to see some movement near the riverbank above: a blur of pink that resembled, oddly, a moving azalea bush.

"Baby," Buford was calling out, "we got visitors."

"Visitors?" a girlish voice responded from the fog. "Not, I hope, the Armadillo Gang."

Under the ramp, August discerned a modestly sized sailboat wedged in the tight channel between the floating wharf and the tangle of rotting wooden foundations behind it. The vessel was far from new: the fiberglass cabin and deck were dented and scraped, the rivets around the window frames were rusted, the weathered timbers of the wooden hull were flaking like bark. The hand-painted script fading on the stern proclaimed the boat's name to be *Sea Hag*.

August's nostrils detected an acrid, vinegary odor that

reminded him of Belladonna's pasta lacquer. On the roof of the low-slung cabin, wrapped in a thick woolly scarf, and with her naked heels resting on the forward hatch, perched a young woman August had met before: Buford's girlfriend, Destiny. Pink dreadlocks fell across her face as she painted her toenails with an eggplant-colored polish.

"Oh, my Lord!" she said, looking up. "If it isn't the little goth and her helmet fella. Look, girl, check it out!"

She rose and pulled aside the scarf to reveal her left shoulder blade, from where an impressive likeness of Claudette extended ghoulish fingers.

"I knew you'd make a great tattoo, girl. Since Buford did it," Destiny said, grinning, "it's been the most requested design in the studio. You're a big hit!"

Claudette, with a coy leer, hugged her dismembered arm with the other and wiggled her hips excitedly.

"Now, get yourself aboard, girl. Bring your friends."

Destiny reached out a limp hand to the ragged troupe.

"Welcome aboard. Like that turban! How you doing that trick with your arm, girl? Jeez, sir, your hand is freezing. That's right; down there. Careful on the steps. Through the galley and into the saloon. Not quite so many butterflies if you don't mind. It's pretty small."

The cabin interior was indeed compact, and dated, but clean and cozy. August and the zombies stumbled through a tiny built-in kitchen into the space beyond, squeezing themselves behind a laminated table into a U-shaped vinyl banquette.

Destiny found herself tightly wedged between Jacques LeSalt and Sad Celeste. She regarded one and then the other with undisguised wonder.

"I have never seen," she marveled, "such impressive makeup. The dead eyes. The loose teeth." She gently touched the exposed radius bone of Celeste's forearm, frowning.

"Now, what in the world," wondered Buford, who leaned on the kitchen counter, his enormous frame blocking the doorway behind him, "brings you to this seedy part of town?"

August explained that they were still in search of the gemstone that had led him to Buford's tattoo parlor the previous summer.

"You know, the Cadaverite, commonly known as alligator's eye? A ball gazer told us we might find it on Pelican Wharf."

"Some ball gazer," Buford said with a scoff. "Any local knows that this is Armadillo turf. Don't they, baby?"

Destiny nodded.

"We pay the gang a little something to moor here," she explained absently, "so they let us be. But I don't know who in their right mind would send kids here after dark. Is that eyeliner waterproof?" she asked of the small, sad-eyed prince.

"Well, they're safe now with us," Buford said reassuringly to his girlfriend. "Hey, who of y'all is partial to hot cocoa?"

August alone raised his hand as Buford lit a stove burner.

"No one else? Y'all look like you could use a little warming up."

"I don't think," said August with a tight smile, "there's any warming up my . . . companions."

Destiny's palms smacked the table with uncharacteristic vigor.

"Wait a minute! Wait one hot minute!" she said with a look of revelation. "The bleached bones. This half-a-face thing. The faint odor of decomposition." Her mouth opened, half smiling. "It's not makeup, is it? Y'all are real live . . . I mean real dead zombies."

She looked sharply at August for confirmation. He paused, then nodded reluctantly.

Destiny clasped her hands together in thrilled disbelief.

"You hear that, baby?" she said. "Zombies! Right here on our little *Sea Hag*." She excitedly grabbed the closest zombie wrists available, one on either side of her. "I am such a fan," she gushed. "Every zombie book. Every zombie movie. You name it, I have most decidedly seen it. Twice. Or more times. I can't believe it. Zombies! Yay!"

Overcome, the young woman grinned at Sad Celeste, then Jacques LeSalt. As she excitedly shook their scrawny wrists in her gripping fists, the two zombies jiggled helplessly back and forth like marionettes, and something dropped from the brim of the pirate's hat. It rolled across the table and toppled on its side. It was a large gold coin.

"Oh, no! Oh my!" cried August, standing swiftly. "We stole from the Armadillo Gang. We need to give that back. They'll come after us!"

"Relax, bro," said Buford, warming milk in a pan. "They are a greedy bunch, to be sure, but they won't miss one doubloon. If you're that concerned, just eat it."

"Eat it?"

"Why not? They're delicious."

August lifted the coin to discover that it was formed from foil-wrapped chocolate. He took a bite.

"Hmm. No Mudd Pie, but it's not bad." He stuffed the rest of the not-so-bad chocolate coin in his mouth. "So, let me get this straight," he said, chewing. "This dangerous Armadillo Gang steals money . . . made from chocolate?"

"Never," said Buford sternly, "underestimate the things some folks will do for chocolate." He moved toward the table with two steaming mugs. "The Armadillo Gang is notorious for its ruthless obsession. It's said they'll stop at nothing to stockpile the stuff, and Carnival is prime time for their thievery. Speaking of chocolate . . ."

Buford placed a mug before August and offered another to Destiny.

"Thank you, baby. Mmm, that's good. I'm warming up now."

As Destiny unwound the woolly scarf from her neck, a

necklace was revealed. It had a distinctive design, being formed from penne pasta lacquered in black.

August gasped.

"That necklace, where did you get it?"

"Do you like it?" Destiny looked down and fingered the jewelry. "It's an original Belladonna Malveau, you know. It wasn't cheap."

"Where did you buy it?" repeated August.

"From this dreary little place in town. Galerie Macabre. Isn't it irresistibly depressing?"

CHAPTER 27

SAINT-CYR'S WAX MUSEUM

The cabin windows were filled with late-morning light and the *Sea Hag* was rising and falling, tossed on choppy waves. They were clearly on a more exposed stretch of the river.

August pushed himself into a sitting position and rubbed his eyes. Claudette was patiently waiting beyond his feet on the banquette. The other zombies were lined along a bench on the other side of the saloon.

"They've been like that all night," said Buford from the galley, turning something out of a cast-iron pan. "They're pretty low-maintenance, huh?"

August became aware of a mouthwatering smell, sweet and buttery.

"Unless," the boy muttered, swinging his feet to the floor, "they're stuck to you like flies to honey, twenty-four seven."

A disheveled Destiny emerged from a small door in the bow, and August glimpsed a rumpled double berth tucked into the space beneath the foredeck.

"Morning," she mumbled sleepily, brushing dreadlocks from her face. "Golly, it is much warmer today, isn't it? Mmm. Do I smell pecan waffles?"

She did.

"Here you go," said Buford, placing an overloaded plate and syrup jug on the table, and squeezing himself with some difficulty into the banquette.

"We're halfway back to town," the huge man explained, spearing a waffle and plopping it onto his plate. "Just stopped for a bite, but we should have you back to the Old Quarter in an hour or two. Save you that long walk."

August, mouth already full of sweet, syrup-smothered goodness, offered a muffled, "Thank you."

He turned to Destiny, swallowing. "Do you happen to have a mirror?" He glanced at Claudette. "I need a reflective surface to try something out."

Destiny shook her head.

"Sorry, fragile things don't last long"—she smiled at Buford—"when you have a giant on board."

Buford threw his girlfriend an embarrassed grimace.

"But I do," said Destiny, "have something else for you."

She fished a business card from her robe pocket and pushed it across the table.

"Here's that address you wanted."

" 'Galerie Macabre,' " read August. "Belladonna thought the name was something like Gallery Macaroni or Macramé. Galerie Macabre; this *has* to be the place."

* * *

"I don't understand," said August. "This isn't an art gallery."

He gazed up at an imposing building of flaking gray stone whose lofty windows and slender Greek pillars occupied the entire city block. A grand, covered entrance protruded over the sidewalk, almost to the curb. Each of its hefty posts bore a vertical crimson-and-gold banner emblazoned with theatrical signage that read "Saint-Cyr's Wax Museum: the famous and infamous, large as life in wonderful wax!"

August pointed to an oval ceramic plaque set into the masonry, high on the building's façade.

"Look!" he said. "This is the old Theatre Français. Here's Funeral Street on the corner." He checked the business card that Destiny had given him. "We have the right address. Where is Galerie Macabre?"

August shepherded the zombies beneath the portico and

approached a heavily carved, dark wooden booth set between two sets of stairs ascending into the building. Behind the box office glass, a rosy-cheeked cashier awaited with an expectant grin.

"We meet again!" cried Cyril Saint-Cyr with delight. "All ready for the Grand Parade, I see. Oh, it's you!" he chided Sad Celeste with a waggling finger. "My, that was quite a stunt you pulled yesterday, young lady—frightened my tourists half out of their wits. Me too, I reckon. The flies were a dramatic touch. I might have guessed you were associated with this colorful group. Now, are you folks all members of an amateur theater society? You certainly commit to those costumes."

"Mr. Saint-Cyr," August interrupted, pushing the business card through the gap in the window, "we're looking for this gallery."

"Well, you've come to the right place." Saint-Cyr returned the card. "Galerie Macabre is the name of our very own museum gift store. It's inside! As you might imagine it would be."

"Oh! Good. I mean . . . how much are tickets?" August fished around in his pockets. "I'm not sure I have enough for all of us."

"Phftt!" Saint-Cyr checked his watch. "We're closing early for the Grand Parade today, in twenty minutes or so." He waved his hand toward the staircase left of the booth. "Come in, come in. It's on the house. And you, feather girl: leave my tourists alone!"

* * *

The airy foyer, with its fluted columns, ornate moldings, and fancy carpet, reminded August of a palace throne room.

The elegant space, once bustling with gentlefolk in evening wear, stood empty but for two completely circular settees of embroidered fabric that used to be blue. From the center of each towered an oversized vase brimming with porcelain flowers, many of them chipped or broken.

Perched on one of these seating arrangements, an academic-looking gentleman with a cat on a leash was reading a book. When August and company ascended the staircase, he emitted a guttural grunt of disgust and removed himself to the obscured side of the settee.

On the far side of the foyer lay three curtained doorways. Only one pair of draperies, however, stood open, and gesturing into the space beyond was an old-fashioned footman in a powdered wig. The man's glass eyes did not blink. His cheeks and forehead had a dull, lifeless sheen, like that of a candle. His ingratiating smile was forever frozen . . . in wonderful wax.

Beyond the drapes lay the soaring space of an auditorium, now home to the Saint-Cyr wax museum. Both had seen better days.

Far above, the gods and cherubs who peered down from a frescoed ceiling were defaced by a mess of gaping cracks and blank plaster patches. The four grand balconies, stacked like layers of a cake, lay in darkness, gathering cobwebs. The stiff replicas of historical figures, athletes, and movie stars were faded and dull, their costumes moth-eaten, the entirety covered with years' worth of dust.

The waxworks were grouped within a series of compact sets, the partitions arranged in such a manner that the visitor was forced to follow a predesigned route through history's most sensational and grisly incidents.

A wild-eyed Emperor Nero strummed a stringed instrument while the ancient city of Rome burned behind him. Mary, Queen of Scots, bared her slender neck for a hooded ax man. A tidal wave of molasses loomed over the scrambling townsfolk of Boston.

They passed into a section entitled "Local Lore," where the displays depicted the more grisly folktales of Croissant City. Jacques LeSalt was there, standing before a noose on the gallows, surrounded by jeering townsfolk. There was even an effigy of Orfeo DuPont, brandishing his wand in a mock-up of the salon in 591 Funeral Street, or, as it was described in the signage, "The Zombie House."

A few feet farther on, August cried, "Hey, look! There's the small prince."

A lavish scene depicting an exotic bed chamber draped in silks and strewn with donut-shaped cushions contained a dramatic and disturbing tableau. A figure lay awkwardly upon the Persian rug, clearly having toppled from a nearby ottoman. His little silk-shod feet stuck straight into the air. His little hands were clasped against his ribs. His little face, although bug-eyed, beet-red, and frozen in a clownish expression of extreme glee, was clearly a likeness of August's smallest sidekick.

"Good Lord," said August. "What's going on here?" He leaned in toward the corresponding informative placard.

"The grandest house on Dolphin Street has long been called the Prince's Palace after its most famous tenant. The visiting dignitary was rich but small, earning him the local nickname of Little Prince Itty-Bitty." August glanced at the pint-sized royal, who confirmed this information with a vague, lopsided smile.

"Upon his arrival to the city," August continued, "with a retinue of servants, musicians, and an elephant, Little Prince Itty-Bitty and his luxurious lifestyle fueled much Croissant City gossip. It was widely known that the prince had a fondness for jokes, especially his own. But this seemingly harmless quirk would prove to be the young person's undoing. Tragedy struck when the prince, attempting to deliver a joke of his own creation, was overcome by a fit of laughter so violent and extended that he promptly dropped to the floor, quite dead. Eyewitnesses lamented that they never even heard the punchline."

* * *

"First Jacques LeSalt," observed August as the group mounted a short staircase onto the old stage. "Then Sad Celeste. Now we have Little Prince Itty-Bitty."

He regarded the well-dressed half-faced lady.

"So, who, I wonder, are you?"

The zombie's exposed jawbone quivered, causing her teeth to chatter. But if there was a response in there somewhere, it was not one that the boy could comprehend.

Up on the stage, the exhibits were given over to a horror theme. Beyond the clusters of wax vampires, mummies, and cauldron-stirring witches, a distinct space had been defined with three freestanding walls. High up at the back, a wide purple sign with black letters in a creepy font read "Galerie Macabre."

"No wonder," muttered August, "Aunt Orchid and all her private detectives couldn't find this place."

The gift store's shelves and stands were sparsely stocked with a thin selection of morbid merchandise: Saint-Cyr's Wax Museum T-shirts with lettering dripping in blood, skeleton bobbleheads playing jazz instruments, and books about Croissant City's ghastly, ghost-riddled history.

At the center of it all stood a glass counter, inside which was displayed a collection of jewelry, all fashioned from pasta and lacquered in black.

August nudged Claudette and pointed to a closed door deep within the shadows of the wings at stage left.

"That," he said in hushed tones, "must be the prop room, where we found these guys, Orfeo's zombies." He scanned the gift store shelves. "If the Zombie Stone is here, it must have been close enough to bring them back to life."

The boy's gaze suddenly stopped short. It had fallen not upon the coveted jewel, but upon a reflection—a reflection of Claudette DuPont.

Upon the counter stood a small oval mirror. It was hinged, so that any face, no matter its height, might determine if it was suited to Belladonna Malveau jewelry. From the glass gazed the girl that August knew from an old mantel photograph in Locust Hole, the girl from the Pelican Wharf puddle.

But, undistorted by ripples and rusting metal, her pressed garments, healthy complexion, and shining eyes were crystal clear. The collar of her dress and wisps of her hair wafted upward, as if she were underwater, or standing above a subway grate.

"Claudette!" breathed August, in wonder. "You . . . you're so . . ."

Gently, he pulled the small zombie closer to the mirror, so that her reflection grew larger. He could see tiny freckles on her nose. He smiled. Mirror Claudette smiled back.

Beside him, zombie Claudette gurgled and groaned.

Before him, simultaneously, mirror Claudette spoke.

"Say it again," urged August. "Louder."

And this time, there was no mistaking it.

"Pearls," said mirror Claudette, with a slight echo, but clear as day.

"Pearls? Are you upset that I sold your necklace?" August glanced at the zombie, then back to the mirror. The young girl was obviously trying to communicate, and August desperately wanted to understand.

"Was it a gift from your brother Orfeo? I can try and get it . . ."

"Ah," cried a voice, causing August to start and turn. "The Belladonna Malveau collection; you have good taste I see."

From behind a balding werewolf, Cyril Saint-Cyr had suddenly emerged, and at August's startled expression, he explained reassuringly, "Oh, I've closed up the ticket booth. I'm all yours."

He glanced again at his watch.

"But we must proceed swiftly, my friends; the Grand Parade begins in just over an hour. Would the young lady care to try something on? Is it not all just so irresistibly depressing?"

August glanced regretfully at the mirror, wishing he had more time to quiz Claudette's reflection.

"No, thank you, Mr. Saint-Cyr. We're actually looking for a sculpture that was sold to you in error."

"In error," cried Saint-Cyr. "Oh, how dreadful!"

"Dreadful. Yes. The model depicts a skeleton boy being carried off by a balloon, the balloon being formed by—"

"By a large amber marble?" interrupted Saint-Cyr.

"Why yes, sir. Yes, that's it! You have it?"

"Why, this is most extraordinary, dear boy," said Saint-Cyr with an air of wonder. "I purchased that sculpture down in Hurricane County last year. And while I found it dismally charming, I'm afraid it has gone entirely without remark or interest for several months. And yet, you are the second party to have inquired after the thing in as many days. Can you believe I sold it just yesterday afternoon?"

August clapped his hands to the sides of his helmet.

"Do you know who bought it?"

"Oh, dear boy." Saint-Cyr's concern seemed heartfelt. "You look like a close friend has just passed away. This sculpture must mean a great deal to you. But I'm afraid this is just a museum gift store. We don't keep records. And it was a cash sale. All I can tell you is that the buyer was a lady, a rather sturdy one, but unremarkable.

"Well, other than her hat of course.

"It was an elaborate thing, so flowery, I recall, that it resembled an azalea bush!"

CHAPTER 28

A SUNKEN PIRATE SHIP

"Did you see her," August asked Claudette, "down near the Pirate's Sea Cargo warehouse? Near the train tracks? The lady in the car, with the hat? Looked like an azalea bush? I thought I maybe saw her again on the Pelican Wharf ramp. Weird coincidence, isn't it?"

But Claudette was distracted by the discovery that she could scratch her back with her severed arm.

August and his zombies hovered in the late-afternoon shadows of Funeral Street. August was ducking his head this way and that, trying to observe the Malveau townhouse through a trickle of pedestrians headed in the same direction.

"Keep still," said August, "here they come."

The front door opened to release Orchid and Belladonna.

Orchid was attempting to adjust Belladonna's hair clip, but the girl swatted her mother's hand away with irritation. They were closely followed by three boy-sized pirates. Beauregard and Langley were amusing themselves, poking the backside of a protesting Gaston with their swords.

"Okay, coast clear," whispered August urgently as the Malveau party disappeared down the street. "Let's get these guys back into the carriage house." He patted a tube of bubbles protruding from his coat pocket. "While they're distracted, we'll lock them in and head to the parade."

He shrugged with an air of hopelessness.

"Who knows? Everyone says that *everyone* goes to the Grand Parade. Maybe the azalea bush lady will too. The top of a float seems a better place than most to try and spot her."

A pleasant thought—unusual—crossed August's mind.

He smirked, nudging Claudette. "I can't believe I'm going to meet the real Officer Claw."

After herding the zombies across the street, August assembled them beneath the townhouse gallery. With the keys he had been given by Escargot, he unlocked one side of the large wooden gate, pushed it open, and then peeked into the passageway beyond.

Through the parlor's side windows, he spied the toady butler heading up the staircase. Then he was gone. No movement.

"Now!" hissed August, grabbing Little Prince Itty-Bitty's arm.

"August, sugar!" cried a voice. "You are running late!"

Champagne Fontaine was, as usual, trailed by her company of weepy widows.

"Riders," she chided, "should be on the floats thirty minutes before the parade begins. My," she gasped, dabbing at her neck with a handkerchief. "It is unseasonably warm—the reason, no doubt, for all these darn bugs." She whisked her tiny hand at August's butterflies.

"I . . . I'm . . ." August had been caught completely off guard. "I'm just dropping off my friends and then . . ."

"Dropping them *off?*" Champagne gave August a forceful little shove. "Why," she cried, oblivious to Claudette's caution-ary growl, "I have never seen in my entire life a more forlorn and bedraggled group of characters. Who better to grace a sunken pirate ship? Your clammy friends must, I say they *must,* ride on the Weepy Widows' float. Don't you agree, widows?" She glanced over her shoulder. "They agree," she added, before any-one could respond.

"Now come along, my dears." She firmly locked arms with Jacques LeSalt and the half-faced lady. "Let's get you into that parade!"

* * *

If previously it had felt to August that the entire nation was fill-ing up the streets of Croissant City, it now seemed as if the entire population of the world had arrived there. Even a couple of days in the bustling Old Quarter had not prepared him for the deafening, overwhelming press of people that had gathered for the Carnival Grand Parade.

Champagne Fontaine, however, seemed entirely undaunted, and barreled through the dense, boisterous mob like an Arctic icebreaker.

August desperately propelled the zombies in the wake of the woman's robust frame.

"No entry!" protested a police officer. "This is the staging area."

"Champagne Fontaine," responded Champagne. "Primary sponsor of the Weepy Widows' float!" She barged past the woman and ushered August, the zombies, and her fellow weepy widows through an opening in the steel barricades.

Here the crowd thinned out, and August discovered himself on an avenue far wider than the cramped thoroughfares of the Old Quarter and lined by stately palm trees and grand old buildings: department stores, hotels, movie theaters. Shining tracks ran down the center of the street, but the scarlet streetcars that they guided sat silent and still, retired for the duration of the parade.

August ogled openmouthed as Champagne bustled the group down a line of Carnival floats, each more elaborate than the last. The giant head of a jester—the size of a candy store—

protruded from a cloud of balloons and flowers. An enormous golden crown was suspended over two velvet thrones in which sat the king and queen of Carnival, robed in white feathers. A girl dressed like a shrimp danced to pop music in the open jaws of a forty-foot alligator, its translucent silver hide lit with neon bulbs from within.

The only indication that these towering, fantastical creations were in fact designed for transit lay in the chunky tires peeking from beneath foil fringing near the asphalt, and in the pervasive vibrato of idling engines.

"Here we are," announced Champagne. "All aboard!"

They had arrived at the largest, most elaborate, and, indeed, most beautiful float that August could see.

Silhouetted against the fading sunlight, an old-world schooner, resting at a distressed angle, was wrecked upon a handcrafted coral reef encrusted with starfish. A large skull and crossbones drifted from one of the two towering masts. Papiermâché sea creatures bobbed about on stiff wire supports, and gauzy fabric, ragged and green like seaweed, fluttered around the rigging, all to suggest that the tableau was an underwater one: a sunken pirate ship.

Gaston and Langley were already engaged in a sword fight on the main deck.

Beauregard, clambering awkwardly up the rigging, glanced

down nervously. But upon spying the DuPonts, the boy's expression twisted into one of revulsion.

The female Malveaus stood near the float's mounting steps. At the sight of August's undead entourage, Belladonna grimaced sympathetically, and Orchid's eyebrows arched with something between disdain and amusement.

"Well, nephew," said Orchid coolly. "You've clearly been busy, but have you found me the—"

But Orchid was interrupted by the abrupt and unexpected appearance of Cyril Saint-Cyr, who you will by now have gathered was prone to abrupt and unexpected appearances.

"At last," he cried, although logically, he himself must have only shortly ago arrived, "the guests of honor! And your theatrical friends from Lapland. Madame Fontaine tells me that she must have you all on board. And who can blame her? Such impressive costuming. Severed arms. Exposed bones. Butterflies. You have it all!

"Come, come. Hurry along now. Up the steps. Excuse me, Madame Malveau." Saint-Cyr nodded, smiling busily at the lady while bustling the zombies onto the float. "We must get the competition winners in place.

"Now, you two, do you remember the instructions regarding the grand marshal? Please do focus," he added as Claudette gazed around absently, enchanted by a cluster of soapy globules

descending around them from above. August looked up to see Beauregard's elbow working hard as he operated the crank of a bubble machine installed in the crow's nest.

"Um." August nudged the zombie to restore her attention. "Yes, sir. Call him Mr. Claw. Don't talk about dogs or llamas. And . . . um . . ." He twisted his mouth, searching his memory.

"No sudden movements!" said Saint-Cyr categorically. "Got that?"

August nodded.

"Good," said Saint-Cyr. "Because you'll be sitting right beside him."

CHAPTER 29

THE GRAND PARADE BEGINS

August's zombies were uncooperative when it came to being distributed across the sunken galleon, returning repeatedly to hover in August's orbit.

"The whole theater group," August explained apologetically to Cyril Saint-Cyr, "is from Lapland. They are thrilled, of course, to be here for Carnival, but none of them speak English, so they'd rather stick close to me."

"Well," muttered Saint-Cyr with some small level of irritation, "there isn't much room up front. But I suppose they can be accommodated here."

Saint-Cyr indicated an area on the foredeck behind three silver-framed chairs upholstered in aqua velvet. Although the ship was angled slightly forward and to one side to suggest its resting position on the sea floor, the seating had been installed on a level platform, for the sitters' comfort.

In the portside chair sat a stocky man with a rather squished-down face, not entirely unlike Officer Claw's.

"That's Claw's handler," Saint-Cyr whispered to August. "Farfel Katz."

On the central chair, raised several inches above the others to indicate his distinction, sat a large but stocky cat with a rather squished-down face, not entirely unlike Farfel Katz's.

Between his ears was perched a tiny tricorn hat secured by an elastic chin strap. Around his rotund torso was wrapped a broad belt fitted with a cat-sized cutlass. He did not look impressed at having to wear a costume.

"That's him," hissed August, gripping Claudette's dismembered arm with unrestrained excitement. "Stella Starz," he babbled, "has groomed that fuzzy tail with her stepmother's toothbrush!"

"Now you, as the competition winner"—Saint-Cyr ushered Claudette into the empty third chair—"sit here."

Officer Claw and Farfel Katz both turned their heads to regard the zombie with something between curiosity and alarm. Officer Claw drew slightly back, his eyes grew enormously round, and his expression resembled that of someone who had just been presented with a bowl of writhing snakes.

August squeezed into position between Claudette's chair and Jacques LeSalt's obstructive undead body.

Immediately in front of Officer Claw's chair lay a square hole in the float's decorative shell. Inside the skeletal cavity just below them, August could see a bald head and meaty knuckles gripping a steering wheel. A friendly face glanced up and smiled. A fleshy hand waved.

"I guess," August whispered in Claudette's ear, "that's the float's driver."

"Congratulations again on your win," said Saint-Cyr, taking his leave. "Enjoy it. Watch out for me on Dolphin Street; I'm commentating for CCTV. I'll be in the balcony with all the lights and cameras, opposite the Yuko Yukiyama stage. And remember . . ."

"No sudden movements," said August.

One after another, the floats in front of them began to move. And, with a small lurch, the sunken pirate ship was off.

Through the flurry of bubbles, August eyed Officer Claw's ample back and rakishly tilted pirate hat with awe. The cat had edged to the left side of his chair and was casting uneasy looks at Claudette on his right. August could scarcely believe that he and Stella Starz's cat were breathing the same Croissant City air.

How, he wondered, might he express his admiration to the grand marshal? He might congratulate him for throwing up in

Hedwig's favorite bunny slippers. He could applaud him for rolling in flour and posing as a ghost cat to frighten off a burglar.

Probably, he should thank him for his ability to make his owner, Stella Starz, smile even in her darkest hours.

The boy leaned over Claudette's shoulder.

"Mr. Claw?" August, heart racing, was surprised to hear the words come out of his own mouth.

There was no reaction.

"Mr. Claw?"

The cat's right ear turned slightly in August's direction.

"I just wanted to say, Mr. Claw, sir." August gulped. "That I think you're a shining example to feline-kind across the universe."

At this generous compliment, Officer Claw turned his head just a little, enough to catch a glimpse of the fluttering carousel of butterflies, and suddenly August had his full attention.

The cat's saucer-like eyes swiveled from left to right and up and down as he observed the twitchy, quivery, mouthwatering buffet of butterflies circling August's helmet.

Officer Claw began to purr.

"He's purring," August hissed in Claudette's ear. "That's a good thing, right? With cats? Oh, my Lord, Claudette; I made Officer Claw purr. Stella Starz's cat likes me."

The boy's heart felt warm. August DuPont, a nobody from Locust Hole, was liked by Stella Starz's cat.

It was the happiest thought that August had had in months. Until he had another.

"What if . . . no . . . but what if Stella Starz is here, watching the parade? What if I meet her? It's possible; I never imagined I'd meet Officer Claw. I never thought he might like me. And anyone that Claw likes, Stella likes too."

August beamed ear to ear, giddy with imagined possibilities. Might he really meet Stella Starz? Might she shake his hand, maybe even like him?

The float lurched, forced to briefly mount the sidewalk in order to maneuver its masts around the horizontal arm of a traffic light as it turned left onto Dolphin Street.

It was here that the parade proper began, and suddenly August was surrounded by kaleidoscopic turmoil. This was a narrower passageway, where the sidewalks were lost beneath the colorful crowds jammed between the buildings and the control barriers on either side of the moving floats. Wide-eyed, August regarded a bustling sea of yelling, drinking, laughing painted and masked faces.

Many of the revelers wore skeleton costumes, elaborate hats, bizarre wigs, or giant heads, and almost all were heavily festooned by string after string after string of the ever-present rainbow-hued beads. Bobbing above the throng were numerous parasols, plastic whirligigs, and fluffy batons resembling feather dusters. August was not sure if the Grand Parade felt like heaven or hell, or a bit of both.

Up ahead, the procession was disappearing into the blinding, blue-white glare of event lighting and August could hear a fuzzy, electronic voice projected through giant speakers. It grew louder as the float progressed.

". . . to the Carnival Grand Parade," Cyril Saint-Cyr was saying, "brought to you, as always, by Malveau's Devil Sauce; if you can't stand the heat, it must be Malveau's! And I'm joined by star of TV's popular *Absurdly Opulent Homes of the Very Rich and Even Richer,* Dixie Lispings. Well, Dixie, it's a fine night for the Grand Parade, is it not?"

"Indeed, it is, Cyril," Dixie Lispings simpered through the speaker. "Positively balmy. If it weren't so early in the year, I'd call this hurricane weather."

"Why, hush your mouth, Dixie. What a thought. Hurricanes indeed! Let's stick to more pleasant topics, such as this next float."

"Well, Cyril, it's just gorgeous. My notes here say that the pelican before us is an impressive fifteen feet tall. Its feathers are crafted entirely from recycled diapers, and its egg . . ."

"Egg?" interrupted Saint-Cyr, bewildered. "I don't see an . . . Oh, my Lord, why there it is! Just popped right out there, didn't it, Dixie? And what's this? It appears to be cracking.

And someone's inside! Who is . . . oh my! Why, I do believe it's our very own Governor Gateau, hatched from a pelican egg!"

Music—a familiar, virtuoso plink-plonking—was also now audible, and increasing in volume. The buildings on the right gave way to open space, where a hundred yards away or so, on the opposite side of a parking lot, August could see the Old Quarter pier and the mighty hulk of the riverboat, the *Delta Duchess.*

Much closer, on the parade route, another—smaller—temporary stage had been constructed, and was occupied by Yuko Yukiyama. She wore a luminous starfish eye patch, a dress that appeared to be nothing more than a white plastic trash bag, and a shallow-domed hat with foil tendrils that resembled a giant jellyfish perched upon her head. Hammers twirling, the celebrated xylophonist was delivering another crowd-rousing performance.

Opposite Yuko, on the left, Cyril Saint-Cyr and Dixie Lispings had slipped into view, perched behind a console and flanked by studio lights, the camera crew, and a makeup artist. All were crammed onto an iron balcony that, at second-story level, hovered just a few feet above August, Claudette, and Officer Claw.

Beneath the gallery, a tourist shop was doing a brisk trade in Croissant City sweatshirts and Jacques LeSalt saltshakers.

"And now," Saint-Cyr pronounced, "the highlight of the parade. This sunken pirate ship, sponsored by the Guild of Weepy

Widows, is captained by this year's grand marshal. You know and love him from television's *Stella Starz,* whiskered celebrity and global feline phenomenon . . . Officer Claw!"

The crowd erupted. Officer Claw sat very erect, haughtily acknowledging the applause by swishing his tail from side to side. August winced; the cacophony of sound agitated the quiet boy. From the left came Saint-Cyr's amplified commentary. From the right came Yuko Yukiyama's xylophonic symphony. From all around came the clamorous cheering and clapping of four thousand Carnival goers, hopped up on party spirit. They surged against the barricades, foreheads shining, long arms reaching for Officer Claw, palms open. Palm after palm, like a field of fleshy flowers.

"Throw!" they chanted. "Throw! Throw! Throw!"

"In the box," came a deep voice from below.

The driver was looking up through the square hole and pointing upward.

"The throws are in there. That's what they want."

August realized suddenly that from all the floats, hundreds of small objects were arcing through the air to be greedily snatched up by grabby fingers: plastic coconuts, plush toys, sparkly masks.

"It's a Carnival tradition," said the driver, and then repeated, "In the box!"

August noticed that generous storage boxes had been wedged between Officer Claw's chair and those on either side.

Through the cloudy white plastic, he could detect something shiny inside. He unsnapped the lid of the box beside Claudette and lifted it off to reveal a treasure trove of glittering colored beads and familiar foil-wrapped chocolate doubloons.

Suddenly an ear-splitting howl, drowning out even the surrounding din, originated from somewhere behind August's left shoulder, and Jacques LeSalt lunged violently toward the trove of gleaming coins, knocking aside August, Claudette's chair, and, naturally, Claudette.

And I'm sure we can all agree that a large, bellowing, tattered pirate hurling his undead self through one's immediate airspace would fail to meet anyone's definition of "no sudden movements."

CHAPTER 30

THE GRAND PARADE ENDS

Given all the dire warnings, what happened next may not entirely surprise you.

Officer Claw did not appreciate the sudden—and to be fair, quite alarming—incident. Despite his barrel-like proportions, for a moment he resembled the kind of cat one sees perched on a witch's broomstick at Halloween: back stiffly arched, fur vertical, ears flattened, and an expression of general feline outrage.

An unstoppable Jacques LeSalt plundered the plastic coffer, coins and beads flying in all directions like missiles, smacking against anything and everything nearby, such as cats.

Officer Claw, horrified, made for safety with claws extended, taking the most obvious route; the open hatch beneath him.

The scream of a bald-headed driver, shriller than that of a horror movie heroine, was followed by an abrupt and violent swerve of the float to the left and a sickening crunch as its front corner collided with a fire hydrant on the curb.

Now, let us not forget that parade floats proceed at a pedestrian sort of pace, so this was in no way a life-threatening collision. It was, however, forceful enough to produce some undesirable results.

The float's heavy steel undercarriage dislodged the aforementioned hydrant, releasing a geyser of water that in turn blasted off the float's front wheel. The entire assemblage, reef and ship, slumped correspondingly to the front and left, sending August, zombies, and a cat handler sliding into the rail of the foredeck.

Utterly lost in a tangle of chair legs and zombie arms, August could not see what was happening, but he could hear Cyril Saint-Cyr's vivid reportage broadcasting through the loudspeakers.

"Dixie Lispings," he cried, "the Weepy Widows' float has come to grief, right below this very balcony. Why, the riders are tumbling left and right. There's water shooting into the sky. There's a man with a cat on his head.

"Oh, my Lord, Dixie, I believe the mainmast is collapsing. That poor boy in the crow's nest. He's falling right toward the Yuko Yukiyama stage. There sure is a lot of that bubble fluid; it's drenching everyone in sight. At least the xylophone broke that young man's fall.

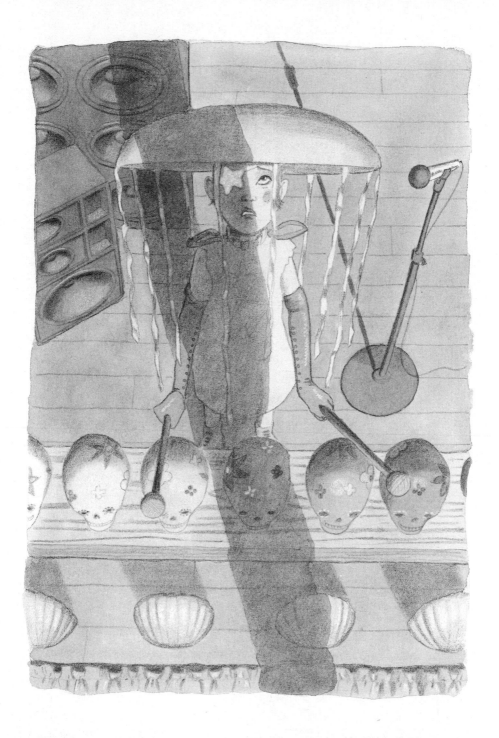

"Oh, and now the foremast is going. It's falling right toward us! Oh, my Lord! Aaaaaargh!"

Dazed, August found himself on the sidewalk, surrounded by chocolate doubloons and general chaos.

Revelers were whooping and dancing in the torrent of hydrant water falling from the sky. Above their heads kicked Langley's feet; he was dangling from the foremast that had fallen against the CCTV balcony. The surrounding loudspeakers emitted only the fizzing and popping of shorting electronics, all commentary and music having ceased.

On the stage beyond the float wreckage, Yuko Yukiyama was dripping slimy fluid from her jellyfish hat and producing clouds of bubbles as she angrily shook her mallets at the pirate boy lying amidst the wreckage of her skull xylophone.

August quickly accounted for his zombies. Claudette was by his side, and he immediately located the half-faced lady, Sad Celeste, and Little Prince Itty-Bitty.

But of Jacques LeSalt there was no sign.

The upended box of Carnival throws rested above August's head, pinned against the foredeck rail. But no pirate. Bracing his shoe sole against the crumpled reef, August grabbed the rail and hauled himself above the surrounding bedlam.

Yards away, moving rapidly toward the river, he spied the pirate's twisted shoulders and lurching gait. The zombie looked around with a puzzled air, apparently disoriented and confused.

His upper arm was in the grip of a fist, which appeared to be dragging him along. The fist was attached to a person wearing a hat, a hat so flowery that it resembled an azalea bush.

And clutched in the flowery hat–wearing person's other fist, held safely above the surrounding turmoil, was a skeleton sculpture set with a large amber marble.

CHAPTER 31

THE MAKESHIFT PERISCOPE

"The Zombie Stone!" cried August. "Headed that way!"

He grabbed Claudette, who grabbed the small prince, who grabbed Sad Celeste, who grabbed the half-faced lady, and they launched themselves into the swelling masses.

August was elbowed and kicked; his feet trodden upon. He was forced to break through linked arms, untangle himself from droopy sleeves, and navigate around large buttocks.

The boy's heart was thundering with a sense of desperation. He could sense the Zombie Stone merely yards ahead of him. August had never wanted anything this badly, so despite his negligible size and weight, the boy forced himself and his comrades through the heaving press of bodies with the inhuman strength of a zombie.

"Can you see them?" he called over his shoulder.

Sad Celeste, tallest of the present party, stood on tiptoe and August plowed in the direction of her sort of pointed finger.

And thus, the pursuers proceeded through the pandemonium that was Croissant City Carnival. August was growing winded, his battery draining. His ribs felt pummeled; it seemed likely to him that by tomorrow he would find bruises on them.

Suddenly his toes hit a low brick wall, and August was face to face with a high iron railing. His zombies, coming in fast behind, crushed him against it. But by clutching at the vertical iron bars, August dragged himself rightward and was released into the wide expanse of an open gateway.

Before him spread a cemetery.

But this cemetery was not the sleepy collection of higgledy-piggledy caskets that constituted the DuPont-Malveau family graveyard on the banks of Black River. This cemetery was a vast, hunkering complex of closely packed stone sarcophagi and mausoleums bisected by a mind-boggling web of avenues and alleyways that were filling with tendrils of the evening mist that, as we've seen, tended to form on the river.

It has previously been noted in this history that by necessity the deceased of this water-logged region were interred above the ground. Where more people live, so more people die, and the resulting arrangements, of tomb beside tomb beside tomb, begin to resemble small cities. So, fittingly, arched above August's head was a metal sign reading "City of the Dead, Number Two."

Whisper, whisper.

But August paid no heed to the now familiar sound; he didn't have time for that.

For deep in the cemetery, an azalea bush was bobbing above the low-lying mist, heading for the river.

"This way!" August half shoved the zombies ahead of him, half dragged them behind him in pursuit of the diminishing pink blur.

The streets traversing the City of the Dead were extremely narrow, only a few feet wide. On either side loomed dark structures in a state of grave decay. Plaster flaked to reveal stained gray bricks beneath. Engraved epitaphs had been weathered to unreadable shadows. Roofs and steps were smothered by moss and lichen. Any unoccupied crevice or gap was choked with weeds and untrimmed palm trees.

The pavers underfoot were broken and uneven. August was stumbling and tripping almost as much as his clumsy companions. And the place was a maze, each claustrophobic lane letting into another, one identical to the next.

The layer of mist was thickening to obscure the surroundings. August stopped, the zombies bumping into him from behind. They were adrift in a pale gray nothingness. The boy's panting swirled the milky vapor before his face.

"We're lost!" He fell back against a mausoleum, attempting to catch his breath.

With all view blocked, August was forced to listen. He heard the distant, muffled hubbub of Carnival revelers. He heard zombie drool drizzling onto the path, the soft *whop, whop, whop* of a passing owl. The cold dampness of the crypt seeped into his bones. The stone seemed to press itself against his spine. Or was the gyration of the planet pressing his spine against the stone? Could he feel a dull, distant throb, perhaps the very heartbeat of the earth?

He had felt this way before, August realized. Once near Claudette's tomb, shortly before her appearance . . . in the proximity of the Zombie Stone. And again, in the prop room of the Theatre Français, shortly before the reappearance of Orfeo's zombies . . . in the proximity of the Zombie Stone.

The boy looked around with a mounting sense of horrified revelation. He was literally surrounded by hundreds—maybe thousands—of corpses, all at this very moment . . . in proximity of the Zombie Stone.

Whisper, whisper.

August was promptly revisited by the dizziness he had experienced while gazing into the Oraculum. Again the whispers gathered, but this time unchecked. Louder and louder they grew, mounting to a steady rush of sound inside his head.

He glanced at Claudette, chest heaving. "You hear it?" She nodded. The other zombies were looking around inquiringly. They heard it too.

The whispers were taking the form of something close to words. They were a thousand voices competing to be heard. But there was more. August could feel a presence, just beyond the horizon of his consciousness. It was a large, swelling presence of many.

It was the Dead.

The boy's heart thundered. He felt fearful and faint.

"Something's happening." He clutched Claudette's shoulder for support. "Something bad. We need to get out of here—right now!"

He looked up, the only point of reference being the stony tomb tops piercing the low-lying river fog. He examined the surrounding vaults but could find no means of scaling them to attain a vantage point.

"Claudette," he whispered urgently, "do your eye thingy!" The zombie cocked her head questioningly. "Take it out," explained August, banging the back of his head and cupping his palm before his face.

The zombie's eyebrows rose in understanding. Using her detached arm, she smacked the base of her own skull, and *plop!* Out shot her right eye. August was ready and, with a grimace, caught it neatly and then handed it back to Claudette.

"Now, hold it up, high." The boy gestured accordingly.

With the extension of her dismembered limb, Claudette's eye cleared the fog and even the press of tombs.

"Can you see the azalea bush?"

She could (while the state of being undead is generally a rather gruesome affair, it does have its advantages).

And so, with the aid of Claudette's makeshift periscope, August and the zombies navigated the City of the Dead Number Two, leaving the whispering, restless tombs behind them and emerging at a second gateway on the opposite side of the cemetery.

The crowds were absent here. Just a handful of smudge-like pedestrians drifted past the formless building before them; a warehouse, August guessed, by its size and elevated windows.

And through the fog, rounding the structure's corner of painted brick, August caught a glimpse of pink. The flower-hatted lady and Jacques LeSalt had gained distance but were still in sight. "Come on!" cried August, finally reaching a space open enough to run.

The boy let his legs go, leaving his shambling undead friends behind, hoping they'd catch up.

He dashed past the colonnaded warehouse frontage and through the surrounding parking lot. He sprinted across train tracks—the same tracks, he figured, that must hug the river, passing through Pelican Wharf and beyond. Then he was racing through a narrow park, over soft lawn, gravelly paths, dodging moss-draped oak trees and couples sauntering hand in hand.

On the far side of a bandstand perched at the edge of the

river, he spotted the azalea bush. Beyond, he could see blurry spots of light suspended above the muddy water—the pier—and at its far end, the illuminated hulking form of the *Delta Duchess*. The deep throb of its mighty idling engine drifted across the water.

August reached the riverbank to find a pair of high-heeled shoes abandoned on the path, and just a few feet below him, the footwear's owner and Jacques LeSalt scrambling down the rocky embankment.

They were headed for a small, aluminum fishing boat with an outboard motor and a hard-top enclosure. The woman, apparently quite strong, hurled the pirate into the boat, where he sprawled across the deck, looking around with confusion and fear.

It was then that August saw it; his model skeleton. It was the best he had ever made, painstakingly crafted from coat-hanger wire and papier-mâché sanded to an ivory smoothness. It depicted a boy dangling from the string of a balloon, but the balloon was an apricot-sized Cadaverite, a vividly beautiful, translucent amber sphere with a swirl of jet-black at its center, reminiscent of an alligator's eye.

The sculpture was cradled in the left arm of the floral-hatted woman, who was, with her free hand, yanking at a rope secured around one of the boulders from which the embankment was formed.

"Stop!" yelled August. "That zombie does not belong to you."

The woman's head jerked up sharply.

Under the azalea branch lay a soft, babyish face, with thick black spectacles and bulbous, pug-like eyes.

"Does it belong to you?" asked a familiar, oily voice.

August peered more closely, and his eyes widened.

"Professor Leech?"

CHAPTER 32

UNDER THE AZALEA BUSH

August, who had started down the embankment, was so surprised that he slipped backward into a seated position.

"It was you? Who purchased the zombie stone?"

"With this disguise," responded Leech, his fingers still tugging to release the mooring, "I had rather hoped to conceal that fact. I have been invited on occasion to conduct ball readings at Saint-Cyr's Wax Museum; I suspected that your so-called Gallery Macaroni was in fact the gift store there."

"Then why," August wondered, "send us to Pelican Wharf? Unless . . . unless you wanted us to run into the Armadillo Gang. Were you trying to . . . to get *rid* of us?"

Leech's bitter leer revealed the accuracy of August's guess.

"Well, get rid of *you* at least," admitted Leech. "There is nothing the Armadillos could have done to this one"—he nodded at Jacques LeSalt—"to render him any deader."

August heard a messy scrambling of footsteps on the embankment behind him, and sensed the clammy presence of Claudette at his shoulder. The zombies had caught up.

"But, Professor Leech, what"—August's voice rose with distress—"do you want with him?"

"What would anyone," scoffed Leech, "want with a two-hundred-year-old pirate?" He leaned forward and with the back of his hand to his mouth he whispered, as if revealing a thrilling secret, "It's the treasure, dummy!"

"But"—August gestured at the pathetic creature attempting to rise on the surging boat—"he's just a zombie; look at him." The pirate at that moment obligingly became entangled in a pile of crawfish traps. "He couldn't tell you where his belt buckle is, never mind find his way through Lost Souls' Swamp to some ancient buried treasure."

"Which is why"—Leech brandished the sculpture—"I required this little trinket. With Orfeo's Zombie Stone, I can revive what little sense of self remains within this bony bag of un-death, and command it to lead me to his long since hidden booty."

"No! He's frightened," cried August, standing and leaping down the stones, closer to the water. "He won't do as you say," August insisted. "Jacques, get off the boat!"

The zombie clumsily attempted to kick free from the crawfish traps, moaning piteously.

Smiling eerily, Leech abandoned the mooring knots, straightened, and thrust his arm and the skeleton boy into the air. The spindly sculpture showed signs of its recent rough journey; its right foot was missing, and its left arm had broken off at the elbow. "Po-Na-Fantom," Leech cried aloud in a theatrical voice. "Ancient talisman. Bridge of Ghosts. Go-between. I call upon thee."

A tiny flickering light appeared at the center of the boy's balloon, as if a firefly were trapped inside.

August was simultaneously revisited by a surge of dizziness and whisperings and the sense of an immense presence nearby and yet far away.

The light within the Cadaverite brightened and expanded, until the whole interior glimmered and sparkled with a flickering spiderweb of luminance.

It was beautiful.

But August's heart lurched with horror, for Jacques LeSalt's eyes had rolled back into his head, and the visible whites glowed with an eerie, milky light.

"Just like the poster," whispered August.

"Spirit who calls itself Jacques LeSalt," cried Leech, "bring me your weapon!"

Gracelessly but without hesitation, the pirate extracted himself from the traps, jerkily crossed the deck, and unsheathed his cutlass. The professor, without turning, reached back to grab the hilt, then swiftly spun the blade toward August.

Its rusty but formidable point quivered mere inches from the boy's neck.

August glanced to his left.

"Her?" laughed Leech. "She can't help you now, boy. Take a look!"

August gingerly (because of the cutlass) turned his head and was shocked yet not entirely surprised to discover that Claudette—that indeed all the zombies—had been reduced to the same trance-like state as Jacques, their awkwardness less awkward, their posture more passive, their eyes burning with that empty light.

"No one," sneered Leech, "can help you now."

With a sudden, violent slash to his right, Leech severed the rope mooring the boat. Carried by the current, the vessel immediately moved away from shore and the man leaped aboard.

Behind him, the *Delta Duchess*'s great red paddle wheel had begun to turn, and the riverboat was pulling away from the pier.

As the gap between them widened, Leech regarded August and spread his hands, one still grasping the sculpture, the other the cutlass.

"You see, boy," he yelled above the din of the riverboat's

splashing wheel. "He with the Go-Between controls the dead! There is nothing you can do to stop me."

August reached into his pocket.

He pulled out the boatswain's whistle.

He lifted it to his lips and blew as hard as he could.

CHAPTER 33

FOLLOW THAT BOAT!

Leech's smile dissolved into a condescending sneer.

Snorting with disdain, he threw down the sword, laid down the sculpture, braced one foot against the washboard, and tugged the outboard engine's starter cord.

A brief snarl petered into a sputtering cough and died.

He tried again with the same result.

A frown creased the professor's brow.

August blew into his whistle again.

And again.

The fog smothered and flattened the high-pitched skirl to some extent; it was not as far-reaching as it might be on a clear night. But it pierced the air sufficiently to send a flicker of alarm across Leech's face.

The professor's efforts to start the boat's engine grew more urgent. But with each violent yank, the motor wheezed, gurgled, and ground, but ultimately stalled.

August blew again. And again.

Leech, now several yards from shore, glanced repeatedly toward the park above the embankment. August guessed that the man was concerned less about the arrival of a small girl on a houseboat than the arrival of a larger and more inconvenient law enforcement officer.

The boy followed the professor's gaze, realizing that for himself, such a development might not be a bad thing. But behind him August discovered only Claudette and the other zombies. They were, at least, emerging from their trance.

Their stances slowly drooped once more. Their awkward manner returned. The glow in their eyes faded, and their pupils swiveled back to loosely fix themselves on August, awaiting instruction.

"Glad to see you back," August assured Claudette, as the hum of another outboard motor became audible.

A hut-like shape was advancing through the swirling mists from the direction of the pier.

"Madame Marvell," yelled August. "Here!"

In moments, the houseboat had passed Leech, and its pontoon was bumping the embankment. August was the last of the group to scramble on board, and, as his first foot hit the deck, there was a throaty, watery roar; Leech's engine fired, and the fishing boat lurched forward.

"Follow that boat!" cried August.

Leech's boat headed downriver, a crest of water spouting from its stern. Beyond it loomed the vast mass of the *Delta Duchess*. Lights high on the riverboat's decks winked weakly in the twilight fog.

The replacement engine from Gardner Island, though dented and unsightly, was powerful, and as a result, the clumsy, stern-heavy houseboat was surprisingly swift.

The unlikely pursuit vessel even began to gain on the fleeing fishing boat.

The riverboat had swung to the right, its immense bulk heading into the river at a sharp angle. The obvious escape route lay through the opening that had appeared between it and the pier, on the vessel's left side.

Leech's boat was headed in that direction.

The houseboat was not far behind, and it was gaining.

August scrambled along the side of the cabin, then threw himself onto the foredeck. On all fours, he clung to the front of the pontoon, bracingly cold water spraying over him as the vessel bounced up and down. Leech, his fist on the tiller, glanced behind him. He and August locked eyes. August thought he saw a glimmer of alarm in the professor's face.

The boy had no idea what he would do if they caught the

zombie-napper. Yes, August had four zombies. But the professor had the Zombie Stone. But maybe, somehow, they could at least get to Jacques LeSalt.

August could not shake the image of the pirate's fear-filled face.

Suddenly, just as it neared the riverboat's stern, Leech's boat veered sharply to the right, plunging across the churning wake created by the riverboat's immense turning paddle.

"Hard to starboard!" yelled August.

But Leech had made a cunning move. Although it lurched dramatically over the foaming ridges, his vessel had a true bow, designed to cleave the water before it. Madame Marvell's houseboat, in the end, was merely a shed roped to a crudely fashioned raft of empty oil drums.

In the violently frothing waves and tall, watery ridges, the houseboat could make no progress, but was spun around, tossed up and down, and thrown side to side. Imagine flinging a shoebox into the river just above Niagara Falls and you'll get the idea.

The creaking craft rolled and pitched, waves smashing on its cabin walls and surging across its deck. An oil drum popped off, compromising the craft's stability even further. Marvell clung to the off-center tiller. The zombies clung to and swung from the ropes that secured the cabin to the pontoon.

But August, kneeling at the very front of the boat, had nothing to secure him. He desperately clutched the edge of the deck, as his knees and feet scrabbled across the boards, sliding this way and that.

Suddenly Marvell's wooden deck chair, Delfine the cloth doll, and a powerful wall of foam were all rushing right at him.

And then August was underwater.

He fared as any person might fare when tossed into a giant washing machine. His limbs flailed helplessly as he was spun around in a violent vortex, until the boy had no idea of which way was up, nor which way was down.

Everything around him was obscured, white with bubbles. The muffled, underwater roar of a giant engine and the thrashing of enormous paddles surrounded him. Suddenly the frothy soup was pierced by something horizontal and rigid and enormous and red that descended upon him.

The next thing he knew, August was falling, slowly. His head hurt a great deal and it was difficult to concentrate. Somewhere high above, he saw a drifting figure—limp, like an old sackcloth doll—silhouetted against the underside of a mighty turning paddle wheel.

He wondered if he was dreaming. Was he still breathing, he wondered, or was he holding his breath? He saw bubbles drifting from his nostrils. Cold, brown darkness was pressing in around him.

To his left, he became aware of a shape emerging from the river's muddy depths. As it grew closer, it grew whiter.

Above him, he became aware of a second shape descending from the water's surface. As it grew closer, it too grew whiter.

The shape on the left was growing very large. Its mouth was opening to reveal rows and rows of sharp teeth and a black yawning gullet beyond.

The shape above had fingers that were reaching toward him.

The fingers were attached to a hand that was attached to an arm that was held by another hand on another arm.

And beyond that lay a familiar face.

"That's Claudette," thought August.

Everything went black.

CHAPTER 34

ZOMBIES ARE PEOPLE TOO

Consciousness returned to August gradually.

He groggily became aware of voices, then the cool silk fabric of the chair on which his head was resting. An impossibly soft blanket encircled his shoulders.

A fuzzy image appeared immediately before him: two dark recesses and a lighter protrusion. It slowly formed into eyes and a nose.

"Welcome back, August," said an unfamiliar voice. A large hand ran over August's head, causing the boy to wince. "That's quite a bump you've got there, buddy. Here." August's glasses were placed upon his face. "One of your friends rescued these from the river."

A young man's friendly face came into focus.

"How many fingers am I holding up?"

"Three."

"And where are you?"

August swiveled his eyeballs. He saw elaborate moldings, square columns, a harp.

"Looks like my aunt's music room."

The hand ruffled his hair. "Good job, buddy."

The face receded, and as the man moved away his paramedic's uniform became visible. He was talking to someone, someone in a long black veil. His voice was hushed, but August could make out some conversational snippets.

"Miraculous he took in so little water."

"You say he was rescued how?"

"And the butterflies are always present?"

"Well, it doesn't look like a concussion but watch for these symptoms."

Above the quietly conferring adults hung the Malveau family portrait. August gazed at it passively, and suddenly realized what it was about the painting that seemed strange.

"Aunt Orchid," he mused, "said her husband died in the Peruvian flu epidemic, the same epidemic that killed my mother . . . when I was a baby. So, the twins must have been babies too, when their father died."

He cocked his head; the children in the painting were around five or six years old. They gazed out of the painting with big, china-blue eyes.

"Did their father not die of Peruvian flu? Wait. The twins don't have blue eyes."

And then it seemed so obvious.

"Those two," he thought, "are not Belladonna and Beauregard."

Looming faces abruptly interrupted his view and his befuddled revelation. August identified the concerned expressions of Madame Marvell and Belladonna. And suddenly in front of them popped a familiar pair of loosely swiveling eyes and a slack, blue-lipped, drooling mouth. August smiled weakly.

"Hello, Claudette." Drips from the zombie's wet ringlets fell into his face. "I guess I should thank you for saving my life."

"It wasn't her," announced Marvell, peering over Claudette's shoulder and clutching a soggy-looking Delfine.

August was beginning to recover. He pushed the blanket away and forced himself into an upright position.

"But I saw her," he said, gingerly rubbing the bump on his head. "In the water."

"It was the alligator," said Marvell. "The great white one, from the swamp. Dragged you to shore by the collar of your coat, I tell you. I swear I'm not inventing a story. Lots of folks saw it."

"It's true," confirmed Belladonna. "Look!"

She swiveled around a laptop computer resting on a small table beside August's chair. The girl jiggled a mouse across the marble, clicked, and the screen was suddenly filled with movement and jarringly clear sound.

". . . why yes, Dixie, that is so." A disheveled Cyril Saint-Cyr and Dixie Lispings were holding mics with CCTV logos. "Many passengers aboard the *Delta Duchess* report having seen an enormous white alligator drag the boy to shore."

The presenters appeared to remain on location. Behind them loomed the wreckage of the Weepy Widows' sunken pirate ship and, beyond, a partly crushed iron balcony. Carnival revelers milled around the edges of the shot, still whooping and toasting the camera with red plastic cups.

"Incredibly, Cyril," responded Dixie, "there is reason to believe that this same young man and his friends were instrumental in bringing about the catastrophe behind us."

A still image filled the screen, one frame, shot by a television camera, that captured the moment of the grand marshal's dramatic exit from the parade.

Officer Claw leaped away in horror from a tangle of lunging limbs. Jacques LeSalt was largely obscured by flying doubloons. Claudette was partly visible. However, the figure closest to the camera, blurry but the most discernible, was August.

"That's right, Dixie," confirmed Saint-Cyr. "Some are calling this the worst Carnival in history. I expect our guests here would agree."

The camera swung slightly to the right to reveal Farfel Katz, Officer Claw, and Yuko Yukiyama. All wore heavy-lidded expressions of displeasure. Claw's tiny hat was crushed. Yuko's jellyfish hat dripped with gooey fluid.

"But none," continued Saint-Cyr, "has a stronger opinion about the matter than this young lady, beloved television actress Margot Morgan Jordan."

The camera swung farther to the right, and August gasped, initially in excitement, but then in quiet horror.

For glaring out of the laptop screen with a furious expression was Stella Starz.

"Now, Margot Morgan Jordan," said Saint-Cyr, a mic suddenly appearing before the young lady's face. "Tell us what you—"

But Margot Morgan Jordan required no coaxing to air her thoughts.

"Loser!" she snapped. "That's what I think. The guy's a loser. No, a monster. Only a monster would traumatize a poor, defenseless cat like our darling Officer Claw!"

From screen left, the large, disgruntled creature in the crushed tiny hat was suddenly shoved into Margot Morgan Jordan's arms.

"Seriously," ranted the actress, "I'd like to—"

The camera promptly cut to Cyril Saint-Cyr and Dixie Lispings.

"Well," laughed Dixie. "No mistaking Margot Morgan Jordan's feelings there."

August felt nauseous.

He shrank back into the chair, wishing sincerely it would open up and swallow him whole.

Stella Starz—world-famous beloved TV star—knew who August was. She had opinions about him. But not in a good way.

Margot Morgan Jordan considered August a loser. No, a monster.

And she was telling the whole world.

August hoped fervently that Cyril Saint-Cyr had not shared his name with Stella Starz, or anyone.

Elegant fingers gently closed the laptop, and the air was fragrant with gardenias.

August, feeling very small, looked up at Orchid Malveau, who seemed very tall.

"I'll look in on him tomorrow," promised the paramedic, heading for the hallway.

But Orchid had turned her full attention to her nephew.

"The stone?" she inquired simply.

August lowered his eyelids and shook his head. He felt worse than ever. He was a disappointment to Orchid. He was a disappointment to Margot Morgan Jordan, better known as Stella Starz.

He was a disappointment to himself.

"He took it," volunteered Marvell. "That man in the flowery hat."

"Professor Leech, ma'am," explained August meekly. "He's using the Cadaverite to make Jacques LeSalt reveal the location of his hidden treasure."

Orchid snorted.

"The greedy fool," she scoffed bitterly, "clearly has no idea of the gemstone's value, or he'd have little interest in pursuing some slimy old doubloons. But that is of little consequence to me."

She stared intently at August.

"For me, this means one thing. No Zombie Stone." Her eyes flickered in the direction of the shabby group huddled aimlessly at the center of the room. "Only, apparently, more zombies."

"Your undead friends, August," the woman said gently, pointedly tapping the closed laptop, "are becoming quite the liability."

August grimaced apologetically.

"That's why," he explained, "I need to find the Zombie Stone—to send them all back to where they came from."

"Ah!" Orchid nodded slowly. "I was under the misconception that the persistence of your search lay in a desire to please your aunt Orchid." She smiled coldly. "But I suppose one must appreciate your position. Undead guests may not always be . . . welcome.

"So, August, what will you do with your dreary friends now?"

"Take them into the swamp; leave them there!" suggested Beauregard's resentful voice.

August noticed his cousin for the first time. The boy stood near the hallway, Langley and Gaston hovering cautiously behind him. Beauregard glowered from beneath his eyebrows with a look of pure animosity.

He had clearly attempted to wipe away the bubble fluid, but his pirate wig was plastered to his head, his pirate makeup was streaking down his cheeks, and his costume was soaked.

"This one," he jerked his thumb at Marvell, creating a tiny flurry of bubbles, "looks like she knows her way around a swamp. She could get you out."

Marvell shot Beauregard a filthy glance.

August, shocked out of his own misery, stood up. "But they would just wander around in there. Lost. Forever!"

"So?" Beauregard shrugged. "They're dead anyway. Wouldn't that solve your problem? Get them out of your hair, and everyone else's?"

August could not help but imagine for a moment what it would be like to wake up with no zombies awaiting him with their unsleeping, googly eyes. No zombies constantly dogging his every move. How much easier, he thought, life would be. No more pursuing the Zombie Stone. No more unsavory incidents. Maybe one day, after people had forgotten . . . friends?

But there was something in the air.

It crept into his being from somewhere outside. It was an emotion, not his own, but he could feel it as if it were.

It was fear.

He looked at his zombies huddling at the center of the room and knew with certainty that they were the source.

"Absolutely not!" he responded firmly, staring Beauregard down. "Zombies can get a little confused. And troublesome; it's true. But they were people once, with feelings, just like you and me. And those people are still in there. Kind of."

August stepped protectively in front of his little horde of un-dead companions.

"These zombies have nothing to fear," he announced, throwing Claudette and the others a small but brave smile. "They will not be abandoned in the swamp. They will not be abandoned anywhere.

"These zombies"—he returned Beauregard's dark and stubborn glare—"are coming home with me!"

EPILOGUE

One hundred and eight miles west of Funeral Street, Hydrangea DuPont lay prostrate on a fainting couch in the parlor of Locust Hole as the local mailman, Mr. LaPoste, poured her a hot beverage.

"Have some fortified tea, Miz Hydrangea," he urged the lady. "It will surely restore you."

"There is no restoring, Mr. LaPoste," wailed Hydrangea. "Not this time. Not after this most cruel and unusual piece of correspondence you have delivered to me today!"

Her arm flailed outward stiffly, and LaPoste extracted a crumpled letter from her trembling fist.

"It's from Pelican State Bank." LaPoste squinted his pale, staring eyes to make out the typeface in the crushed paper. His perpetual toothy smile finally faded. He looked at Hydrangea with a gray, rabbit-like face. "If you don't make a payment toward your loan," he said, "by the last day of June, Pelican State Bank will take possession . . . of . . ."

He bit his lip, unable to say it.

"Take possession of Locust Hole," said Hydrangea, sitting up, eyes welling with tears. "Oh, what will become of us, Mr. LaPoste?" The lady's hands worked her handkerchief. "The bank is going to turn us out of our home, onto the street! Poor, poor August. It is I who should be caring for the child. But I confess, Mr. LaPoste, it is rather the child that has for many a year been caring for me." She covered her face.

LaPoste took a seat beside the distraught woman and placed a hand on her shoulder.

"And there really is no hot sauce left?"

Hydrangea shook her head.

"I just sold the last thirteen bottles to a buyer in Pepperville."

"And there really is no question of reviving production?"

"Why, Mr. LaPoste, I'm afraid I have not set foot outside this house for . . . oh . . . who knows how long?"

"Thirty-five years." LaPoste supplied the number.

Hydrangea nodded absently. "Not since . . . the incident."

"The incident," agreed LaPoste sympathetically. "I remember. I was there."

"How am I to oversee a pepper farm"—she gestured at the boarded-up windows—"from here?"

"You know," LaPoste said gently, "I have a little something put away. It's not much, but . . ."

Hydrangea was horrified.

"No. No, sir! Absolutely not. I wouldn't hear of such a thing."

LaPoste sighed and patted her hand.

"Well, perhaps," he half laughed, "you should do a little grave-digging; it seems there might be some profit in it."

Hydrangea frowned from behind her handkerchief.

"What a suggestion, Mr. LaPoste! Whatever can you mean?"

The mailman pulled a small-format newspaper from his mailbag and, unfolding it, pointed at the front page.

A good portion of it was filled by a photograph of a dapper gentleman beaming behind a table laden with a stack of large, ragged scrolls.

The headline read, "Local man unearths trove of antique maps."

"You remember," said LaPoste, "our old school friend, Jupiter Goodnight?"

"Why, of course, the undertaker's boy. Very well dressed, as I recall. Loved beignets."

"Well, according to the *Pepperville Prophet,* Jupiter's great-uncle Uranus passed away last month."

ocal man unearths trove of antique n

"He was one
hundred and
eleven!"

Jupiter Goodnight of Goodnight's Funeral Parlor

What's with all
the butterflies?

"Oh, how sad."

"He was a hundred and eleven."

"Still."

"As the casket was being interred in the Goodnight family crypt, it seems that Jupiter came across this crumbling stash of maps. One of his ancestors was apparently an avid cartophile. Map collector," he added at Hydrangea's blank expression.

"Well, valuable as they may be," said Hydrangea, "I doubt some old maps would equal the value of Locust Hole."

"Oh," chuckled LaPoste, "it's not the maps themselves that are the real find. Listen to this!"

Straightening the newspaper, the mailman held it upright and read:

> *Pepperville's own librarian, Octavia Motts, suspects that many of Mr. Goodnight's maps are over two hundred years old and depict Hurricane County's coastline prior to the diversion of the Continental River.*
>
> *"But," says Mrs. Motts, "the most intriguing document of all is one that dates from the golden age of privateering and appears to locate a pirate's ill-gotten spoils."*
>
> *Mrs. Motts goes so far as to suggest that the indicated treasure might even be that of fabled folk hero Jacques LeSalt.*

To be continued . . .